REEL STUFF

REEL STUFF

A Novel

DON BRUNS

Oceanview Publishing

LONGBOAT KEY, FLORIDA

ISBN 978-1-60809-096-9

Published in the United States of America by Oceanview Publishing, Longboat Key, Florida
www.oceanviewpub.com

2 4 6 8 10 9 7 5 3 1

PRINTED IN THE UNITED STATES OF AMERICA

Reel Stuff is dedicated to Metropolis Books in L.A. and Mystery Book Store in Westwood. Your doors are now closed, but I have wonderful memories.

ACKNOWLEDGMENTS

Thanks to Mary O'Connor, Hugh Hefner's secretary, for championing my writing and setting up the first movie pitch at Henson Productions, and to Ed Thomas from Book Carnival in Orange County who by his love of the books encouraged me to keep writing. You will both be greatly missed. Thanks to Scott Howell for technical information, to Sue Waronker, Kathy Bavely, and Betsy Timmermeister for becoming characters in the novel. Your donations to charitable organizations are much appreciated.

REEL STUFF

CHAPTER ONE

"Sometimes it's just stupid to do your own stunts." The director let out a long sigh, shaking his head. He looked at me and said, "We've got stunt guys who can do this jump with their eyes closed, so why the hell does this prima donna think he should do it himself? Damned actors. Life would be a lot simpler without them."

And you'd be out of a job, I thought.

Randy Roberts pointed at the steel scaffolding that in the last two days had sprung up around the outdoor soundstage. Seventy feet above us in the full hot sun of a Miami morning, a male actor paced back and forth on the metal framework. The same actor Roberts was railing against. The man would stop, spread his arms like a bird on the wing, then put them down and pace again. Two grips stood on the grating, watching the scene unfold.

Roberts clutched his aluminum coffee mug, nodding to me. "Big Hollywood star, hotshot likes to be able to say he never uses a stuntman. So the risk goes up, we pay a whole lot more for insurance, we've got to have a medical team on hand—" He

1

glanced at the green-and-white ambulance parked in the grass just a few feet away. Two uniformed medics were looking up, waiting for the big moment.

Once again, the actor paused, spreading his arms, looking beyond the sparse crew that was anticipating the shot. The set was guarded, protected from passersby, but a handful of actors, security people, and staff were around to witness the event. After all, the jumper was Jason Londell.

"The bag's fully inflated?" Roberts shouted to a young man dressed in jeans, a T-shirt, and sporting a scruffy beard.

"Checked it five minutes ago."

"Jesus, I wish he'd use a double."

Again he directed his statement to me, as if to overly convince me that he wanted to put a halt to this madness.

Randy Roberts had no idea who I was. I just happened to be the closest person standing next to him, and he was venting his frustration. Squinting as he gazed at the scene high above us, he wiped at the sweat on his face with the sleeves of his shirt. It was only nine a.m., but sweat trickled down the big man's cheeks and his denim shirt had dark circles under the armpits.

Under his breath he muttered, "If I'd slept with the right people in this business, I'd be a lot further ahead."

Always having heard that women slept their way to the top, I found it a strange statement coming from the male director.

My understanding of the shot was that it was to be quick. It was only going to take three or four seconds. Londell was to run a few steps on the scaffolding, turn his head looking behind himself, and dive off, landing safely on the soft cushion of a tethered air bag inflated with helium fifty feet below. The bag was weighted down and so big, I assumed it was an easy target. But what do I know? I get dizzy looking out over a second-story balcony.

A cinematographer with a large, handheld camera was

perched on the catwalk, waiting to capture the action, and another camera mounted to a tripod was about thirty feet from me to get a second angle as the body plummeted to the ground.

Roberts spoke in measured tones, his wireless microphone transmitting to Londell's earpiece.

"Okay, Jason, run, look over your shoulder, then stop. Let's do it at least three times so we get the angles right. I don't think either of us wants you to do the jump multiple times."

From above, the actor nodded.

The camera guy on the scaffolding crouched down, shooting up at Londell.

"Action."

Londell was jogging, not going at any great speed, but there was only maybe thirty feet of room to run. And besides, that metal walkway was very narrow.

The actor glanced over his shoulder and pulled up short.

"Camera one, you set? Ground camera?"

Roberts wiped the sweat from his forehead, pushed his sleeves up even higher on his thick arms, and once again spoke to Londell.

"Okay, Jason, let's try it again. Cameras will roll, but it's just a dry run."

Roberts took a swig of his coffee, rumored to always be laced with a healthy dose of brandy, and nodded.

"Camera one," he paused, his eyes glued to a screen in front of him. On that screen I could see the actor above, ready for his run. "Shoot this one. Okay. Action."

Londell ran, faster than before, almost sprinting, and there was no furtive glance over his shoulder this time. Looking up I watched him veer slightly to his right, throw his hands in the air and leap from the scaffolding, the sun glaring off the metal framework, and for a moment I was blinded. I blinked, not believing I'd actually witnessed the jump, and saw the body, plunging to the earth.

There were shrieks and a wild scattering of the support staff as Jason Londell hurled through the air. The screams grew in intensity when his body slammed into the ground with a sickening thud, roughly twenty yards from where the giant air bag waited.

CHAPTER TWO

I've seen dead bodies, bodies that had been shot, bodies that had been knifed, but I'd never witnessed something as gruesome as this. It appeared the movie star had exploded from the impact. His head was cracked open, and I could see blood and what I could only imagine was gray brain matter. Londell's eyes were open and one orb was dangling out of its socket. Landing on his front, his rib cage seemed to be splayed from the impact and his arms and legs were bent in unnatural positions, white broken bones protruding from gashes in the skin.

Running to the scene with some sort of portable respirator, the two medics bent over the actor, poking and prodding, apparently not convinced that he was deceased. Almost in a trance, I moved into position to do my job. Keep the bystanders at bay.

I'm Skip Moore, and my partner, James Lessor, and I have a private detective firm called *More or Less Investigations*. We were on the set of the television series *Deadline Miami*.

Jason Londell is, or was, an A-list movie actor who had agreed to play a walk-on for one episode, but only one, due to his commitment to the movie industry. He was currently shooting two feature films in California and, with a very small window of opportunity, he was able to fly to Miami and do a favor for his good friend Clint Anders, the producer of *DM*.

How do I know this? I'm not a celebrity stalker but, as a private investigator who is taking every opportunity to make a buck, James and I are listed in the phone book. When the Anders people found *More or Less Investigations* in the Yellow Pages, they sent us a letter explaining that they would be requiring some private security during two episodes of the show. James immediately jumped at the chance.

So we're part of a security team. Providing some safety for the actors. Our glamorous job is to keep street people on Bay Shore Drive out of the park where these episodes of *Deadline Miami* are being filmed.

We get such comments as, "It's my damned park. I live in this city." Or, "I'm going in, and I'd like to see you stop me." And the perennial, "I pay taxes here, asshole." Actually, a lot of the people to whom we'd denied access probably didn't earn enough money to pay taxes. And several of them were panhandlers and, while they probably made more than James and I combined, they didn't pay taxes either.

Along with five other security people, we try our best to protect the set during filming.

In a matter of minutes from the time of Londell's jump, the cops had shown up, the photographers had been there, we were interviewed, and everyone who'd witnessed the event was still shell-shocked.

"We'd like for all of you to stay around for a couple of hours," a tall, lanky detective with a Texas drawl held up his hand and addressed the staff that was still mingling in the area. "Please. There will be more questions, and even though you saw what you saw, we need to have a thorough investigation. Cause of death has yet to be determined. It may take a while to ascertain," he paused, almost pleased with the word ascertain, "the cause of death."

Just what I needed. More questions about the terrible scene we'd all been subjected to. Jason Londell's body crashing to the ground. Blood, bones, and brain in a twisted, gruesome tableau.

The medical team had driven off with Londell in a body bag, and I was never going to get that vision out of my head. The screams from those assembled as the actor vaulted into the air, his arms spread wide, and the sickening thud as his body crashed to the ground. I was sure his broken body was going to be a permanent, horrible memory for everyone who saw it.

James had the morning off and wasn't expected to return until later, but the way stories go viral in Miami, I felt certain he'd come back fully briefed.

I smelled her perfume before I saw her, and right away I knew who she was.

"Oh, my God, James—"

"It's Skip."

"Whatever," she grabbed my arm and sobbed, "this can't be real. He was about to—oh, my God."

"What? About to what?" Confess to a crime? Announce that he was retiring from the movie business?

"I think he was about to propose." The bosomy Ashley Amber was shaking, and even though I thought of her as an opportunist with little talent, the actress's emotions seemed sincere. "Do you believe that? He—" she shut down for a moment, finally raising her head and whispering, "He loved me. He told me last night. We were really connecting, and for him to jump, it just makes no sense."

So the two of them were dating. That was a good enough reason for him to fly to Miami, especially since *Deadline Miami* was picking up the bill and giving him a paycheck as well.

"I'm really sorry, Ashley."

"James," she paused, collecting herself, "do you have any idea what this means? Oh, my God."

As she hugged me, her ample chest pressed into my arm. I'd actually seen her nude in a Jonah Hill movie and felt like I knew those breasts intimately. It was all I could do to keep my focus on the dead body of Jason Londell.

"The name is Skip, and I do," I said. It meant that if he really was going to propose, they wouldn't be spending their lives, in this life, together.

"Pard, what the hell?"

A slightly out of breath James Lessor was actually jogging up to us.

"I just heard it from one of the cooks over at the food tent. So where were you when this happened?"

I pointed to the top of the scaffolding. "They were getting ready to film the jump scene. I was standing over there with Randy Roberts. It was surreal, James. I'll play that over in my head for years."

"What about the inflated bag? I thought this guy knew the ropes. I mean, we were told that—"

"James, he was out of sequence. Roberts called for three takes before Londell jumped. I heard him tell Londell exactly that, 'three takes before you actually jump.' He jumped on the second take. And he had no intention of hitting that bag. He landed a good twenty yards from his goal."

"You saw it? God, Skip. I can't imagine." James nodded to Ashley, acknowledging her for the first time. Her face was wet with her tears, and I hugged her, not wishing this on anyone.

"He called me last night," she said, her brown eyes looking into mine.

"And?" James, trying for some clarity.

"He was concerned about the scene."

"Today's scene? The jump?" I asked.

"Yes."

"What was the concern?"

She brushed her face with the back of her hand. Sniffing and choking on her words, she said, "He is always concerned when he's doing a dangerous stunt."

I felt like telling her what Roberts had said. The company had qualified doubles to do the jump. He didn't need to put himself on the line.

"But the worst thing was—" she paused, looking up at the two men heading toward us.

Bill Purdue, head of our security team, walked up with a tall man in a plain white shirt and loosened blue tie, his sleeves rolled up and aviator sunglasses perched on his nose.

"Detective Hawk, this is Skip Moore. He was on the scene when Londell jumped. Right, Moore?"

I nodded. The hot Miami day was soaring into the nineties, and I could feel heat cooking every inch of my skin.

Hawk flipped on a palm-sized recorder.

"What's your job, Mr. Moore?"

"I sell security systems in Carol City." I don't make many sales and I don't make much money, but it's supposedly my full-time job. I was taking time off for this gig, but in three or four days I'd be back knocking on people's doors, suggesting they may want to buy a system that would secure their meager possessions.

He glanced at Purdue, seemingly puzzled.

"He's temporary." Purdue pointed to James. "He and his friend Lessor keep gawkers away from the set. They do some driving for the actors and act as sort of a buffer between the crew and people on the street. When we're shooting outside, like in this park, we need extra security because we're basically wide open to anyone who wants to approach us."

Hawk nodded. He glanced at Ashley. "And you are Ashley

Amber." There was a glimmer in his eye, as if he was secretly, or not so secretly, pleased that he was interviewing a starlet.

She nodded, brushing at her hair with her fingers.

"Londell called this young lady last night," James said.

Ashley finally let go of my arm, wiping at her damp face.

"You talked to him?"

"I did. He was worried about the jump today."

"And that was the discussion you had with the deceased?"

Life is obviously fleeting. Two hours had passed and someone who was a living, breathing human soul was now referred to as "the deceased."

"So you were close to the actor?"

She took a shaky breath.

"We were dating."

"I will need to talk to you in private, Miss Amber. Questions that may be of a—" he glanced at James and me through the dark lenses, "—of a personal nature. I assume you have some time."

Turning off the recorder, he turned to Purdue.

"You can contact these people if I need to talk to them again?" he asked.

"I can."

"Thank you for your cooperation." Hawk and Purdue walked away with Ashley Amber. The same Ashley Amber who had said, not two minutes ago, "and the worst thing is—"

"Suicide?" James said the word and it almost made me sick. I'd been nauseous several times that day.

"I don't see how it was anything else," I said. Two grips and a camera guy on the scaffolding, a camera down below. Both of the cameras filming the rehearsal, even though it wasn't supposed to be a final take. They would show exactly what I saw. Londell was out of control, failing to follow the director's dictate. And the leap seemed to me to be totally deliberate.

"Damn, amigo, this guy must have had some serious issues.

But what a colorful way to exit. This will be page one on every news outlet in the country. Maybe the world. *Academy Award Winner Leaps To Death*. Too bad he's not going to be around to read his own reviews."

"But we don't have an answer as to why. Why he jumped, took the plunge."

"You know, Skip, I'd love to have an answer. But we weren't hired to solve the crime; just provide security."

CHAPTER THREE

Three in the morning I heard the tapping at our on-location Airstream trailer door. James grunted, rolled over, and resumed snoring. In my boxer shorts, I swung out of my bed, walked the five steps to the entrance, flipped on the light outside, and opened the door. I was staring into the pale face of Ashley Amber, wrapped in a striped blanket, or maybe a serape, her tired eyes staring into mine, hands clutching a designer purse in front of her.

"James."

"I'm Skip."

"Whatever. I need help."

"Okay." I was groggy, not sure where this was going. It appeared she'd been crying, but I didn't feel comfortable prying for information.

"The police, they had a lot of questions. They wanted to know how close we were, what I knew about his life away from the movie business. They wanted to know—"

"Ashley, when they took you in for questioning, you were in

the middle of a sentence. You were talking about your possible engagement and you said—"

"I know what I said. I said, 'the worst thing was.'"

"Yeah. That."

"And you want to know what the worst thing was?"

"I'm a private investigator. It's part of what I do. I ask questions."

"The worst thing was—and I haven't told the police this—when he told me he was concerned about the jump, he said he'd been receiving threatening e-mails."

"He was a Hollywood legend. I would guess that he got thousands of threatening letters, e-mails, texts, postings on Facebook—"

"James," I didn't correct her, "Jason was the most gentle man. He was like a river of peace."

"A river of—"

"Soothing, calm, focused. Someone who took other people's problems as his own. He was getting these messages from Juliana, and she had no reason to—"

"Do you want to come in?" Suddenly, I realized I had this beautiful actress on my doorstep, and I was standing there in boxer shorts.

"Yes."

She stepped into the tiny trailer and immediately removed the wrap. She wore a summer dress that was high above her knees and low on her chest. I tried not to notice as she sat in one of the ratty, green, cloth-covered chairs in what passed as our living room. Actually, our apartment was possibly in worse shape than the Airstream, so for the past three nights, this was a step up.

"Let me get dressed," I said and walked five feet to our small bedroom where James was lightly snoring. I pulled on a pair of jeans and a Green Day *American Idiot* T-shirt, decorated with someone's fist squeezing a hand grenade. Walking back into the living room, I sat across from Ashley, trying not to look up her short dress.

"Who is Juliana?"

"She's a talent agent."

"Jason Londell's talent agent?"

"She was."

"So she's upset that she isn't any longer?"

Ashley pursed her full lips, and I figured as perfect as she looked, she'd probably had a little work done. Maybe some lip plumper or filler. Everything about her was just too perfect.

"She's upset about a lot of things," she said.

"So, have you seen any of these threatening messages? I mean, was she going to sue him? Try to destroy his reputation? Or was she talking about killing him?"

"I haven't seen any of the messages. He told me about them. There was one in the last several days that said, 'Be careful on the set, Mr. Londell. You wouldn't want to have an accident.'"

"That's it?"

"I didn't see it. He only told me that he felt threatened. And now the authorities have his computer and his cell phone. They told me they were going over all that material."

"Why didn't you tell the cops about the threats?"

"I didn't have any proof."

"Well, I'm sure the police will find out if it was a suicide or not."

She shuddered and the start of tears made her green eyes shine.

"I understand that it hurts, but it sure looked like he wanted to take his own life. I saw it firsthand."

"I don't believe it."

The man had jumped off a seventy-foot-high scaffold. With

a perfectly good, inflated air bag on the ground, he'd missed his cushion by twenty yards.

"Ashley, I'm really sorry for your loss."

"Will you take the case?"

"What?"

She pouted, another facial expression from her acting arsenal.

"Will you take the case?"

"What case? There is no case. The man jumped."

Now it was a pout with a frown, except the frown seemed forced, like maybe she'd had some Botox injections and her facial muscles were frozen. But then, I really don't know anything about plumpers, fillers, or Botox. It just appeared that—

"I want you to investigate Juliana. Find out if she did send threatening messages and see if there is any way she could be behind his death."

James and I always needed money. I haven't seen the figures lately, but I'd bet we are dead last in nationwide earned income percentages.

"I just don't see how this could be—"

"Let's hear her out, pard." James had risen from his slumber and stood in the doorway, stretching and yawning. "Don't want to be too hasty. Maybe Ashley has some reason for suggesting this lady, this Juliana, wanted Londell dead."

"She was his agent, and now she's not. Right, Ashley?"

"He fired her," she said.

"We'd need a five-hundred-dollar retainer." James was as blunt as I'd ever seen or heard him.

Ashley Amber reached into her Marc Jacobs ginger-quilted purse and pulled out a checkbook. I know, how would I recognize the purse she carried? My girlfriend, Emily, who lives a pretty good life, owns at least two MJ purses, and the style and quilting are distinctive. I'm embarrassed I even know that, but I do.

"We should talk about this, James."

15

"For five hundred dollars we'll look into it, Skip." He shot me a disapproving look. "If we feel that there's room for more investigation, we'll tell you, Ashley, and agree upon a price. Okay?"

She was already writing a sum on the check.

"Who do I make it out to?"

"More or Less Investigations." James wasn't going to let this one get away.

Taking a deep breath and slowly releasing it, I said, "We're going to need a little more information about this Juliana."

"What information do you need? I know her pretty well."

"Where does she live?" James asked.

"California."

"She's there now?"

"As far as I know. Although, she might be in Miami. I don't keep track of her location."

If she is in L.A., I'm sitting there wondering how she killed Jason Londell long distance.

"She's a talent agent," James continued. "Does she work for a firm, or is she on her own?"

"Independent. She used to work for DDO Artists Agency. Before that, William Morris."

"How do you know her?"

"I've known her all my life. She's my sister."

"Whoa." James took a step back. "I didn't see that one coming."

"Juliana. Does she have a last name?" I asked.

She rose from the chair and handed James the check as he stood there bare-chested in his boxer shorts with bright red rosebuds printed on them.

"Londell."

"Like, Jason Londell?" I looked back and forth to Ashley then to James.

"She's his wife, okay? And she's carrying his baby."

16

CHAPTER FOUR

"You're out of your frigging mind," I told him.

It was eight a.m. and James and I had stayed up most of the night, arguing over the validity of the case.

"You just made two hundred fifty bucks, amigo. Because I decided to take the case. I just made two hundred fifty bucks because I took the case. So how crazy am I?" He swigged a swallow of coffee, staring at me across the small breakfast table, Ashley Amber's check in front of him. He raised his voice even higher, and louder. "It would be nice if *you* would be that crazy. Help *me* make two hundred fifty bucks."

"You know I can damned well use the money just as much as you." The reason we'd taken the original security job was to help pay the rent and another two hundred fifty would be sweet. We were always struggling at month's end to pay the bills. Hell, we were struggling at the beginning and in the middle of the month. He knew I wanted the money, but he also had to realize there were principles here.

"Then let's drop it, Skip. Take the money. We'll run a check on this lady, this Juliana Londell, and we'll see if there was any reason for her to—"

"James, I saw it." I pounded my cup on the tabletop, some of the bitter liquid spilling onto the table. "I watched. Up close. Randy Roberts told him to practice the run three times, then do the jump. Roberts was working with camera angles. Londell ignored the directions, dude. It's as simple as that."

I could hear Roberts's voice telling him exactly what to do. I could relive the entire episode. I could slow it down and watch it in 3D, all in my head. I was there. The actor, Jason Londell, didn't follow directions and he leaped off the metal structure to a certain death. It was deliberate. But the cop with the sunglasses, Detective Hawk, and James, my partner, plus the sexy Ashley Amber, they weren't buying into it. They believed the death might be murder. They seemed obsessed with the idea. Yet I'd never seen anything so plain and simple. Being an eyewitness, having watched the entire incident, I knew without a doubt, the movie star was looking for a way out. It was suicide. Jason Londell took a dive, and it was deliberate. There was absolutely no doubt about it.

And I wished I could get the image out of my head.

"Skip," my roommate seemed exasperated, "this lady seems convinced that Londell was murdered." He threw his arms up. "Convinced. Come on. She's willing to put up money, amigo. And we could use the money."

"You apparently haven't listened to a word I've said, James. I'm not going to discuss it any further. You can keep my half. I know what I saw. It was a deliberate jump. End of story."

My cell phone went off, playing Bruce Springsteen's *Born In The USA.*

"Hello."

"Skip Moore?"

"Yeah. This is me."

"Hey, Randy Roberts here."

The director who I could have sworn didn't know my name. And then I remembered. As security staff we had to give our cell phone numbers to all key personnel. Roberts was key personnel and he'd gone through the list of security employees and figured it out. Or maybe I was number two or three or four on the list he was calling.

"Mr. Roberts."

"Please, it's Randy."

"Okay, Randy."

"You were standing next to me yesterday when Londell jumped. Am I right or am I crazy?"

His words were just a little slurred, and I wondered if he was drinking his coffee and brandy this early in the morning. And he could have been crazy, but he was right about me being next to him. Roberts had made an issue of telling me what he thought of Londell and his desire to perform his own stunts.

"Yes, sir."

"Good, good. Then it is you I was looking for. Listen, I'm going in for questioning this morning."

Questioning?

"They questioned you earlier, didn't they?" These investigators weren't satisfied. They were very pushy.

"Follow-up they called it. Listen, kid," I was convinced the director had been drinking. "I can't imagine what they're going to ask me, but someone has suggested the man was murdered. Murdered. Understand?"

I understood. The man hadn't been dead twenty-four hours and the murder angle seemed to have taken over.

"Did that appear to you to be a murder? You were right next to me. You watched the entire scenario, didn't you? My story is that Jason Londell didn't follow directions, and I never instructed him to jump. Am I missing something here? That's what happened, right?"

"Yes, sir."

"He was up there with the camera guy and two grips. Hell, I was seventy feet below. I didn't notice anything strange until he came out of the sky. Am I right? Come on, you know I am."

The pitch of his voice rose as he spoke, and I detected a real concern. He was begging for confirmation.

"You are. You're right." Saying the same things I had said to James and Amber. Roberts was obviously very shook up.

"You were standing there, remember? I gave him specific directions. Three times he was to run the route. Three times. Then he was to jump onto the bag. Tell me you remember it like that."

"Mr. Roberts, Randy, it's what I heard." I didn't know what else to say. "I've been through these interrogations before. They're just trying to be very thorough. Don't worry about it."

I wasn't so sure myself. Maybe they thought Roberts had something to do with the death.

"All right." He let out a slow breath as if relieved that I was going to tell the whole truth, nothing but the truth, so help me God. "Listen, if I get into a jam, I may ask you to repeat that."

"Excuse me, but what kind of a jam could you get into?" Was I dealing with a criminal? Wouldn't be the first time.

"When the cops asked me for the interview," he paused and took a deep breath, "they said something that bothered me."

"What was that?"

"The officer who called said, 'Since you were the last one to talk to him.'"

"*I* heard what you said. How could that be a problem?"

"You never know. I was involved in an overdose case in L.A. several years ago where a girl died. Reality TV star was shooting up. I was the wrangler, basically herding the talent. Glorified babysitter that job."

"And?"

"I should have been watching her more closely. Girl by the name of Audrey Love. I'd been in her trailer about half an hour before she went down, and those L.A. cops laid on me for two days. Two days, Moore. They were bound and determined to make me a culprit. If the police think there's a case, they go after anyone in the immediate vicinity. Firsthand experience. I've seen it in person." He paused. "Took me a while to get another job after that. This isn't an easy racket."

"I told you, Randy. I heard exactly what you said."

"Thanks, kid. It may be nothing, but I just wanted to make sure I remembered what happened. Got a little shook up about the way that scene ended. Never, ever saw it coming, you know."

Randy Roberts wasn't the only one who'd been shaken.

He hung up and as I pocketed my cell phone, it rang again.

"Yeah?" I answered without checking the number.

"James?"

"No, this is Skip, Amber. Skip Moore."

"Oh. Listen, I just heard something that came down from the coroner's office. I've got a friend who knows someone."

I knew it. She was trying to drag us deeper into this mess, trying to prove her sister murdered Jason Londell.

"And what did they tell you? This friend who knows someone?"

"Apparently, they found a foreign substance in Jason's body."

"Exactly what does that mean?"

"I don't know. They said it was a preliminary report. Nothing they could release just yet. But I do know that Jason didn't do drugs. And I was with him all night until he went on the set yesterday morning."

"Yeah?"

"James, he had a couple glasses of wine. That's all. And the last I heard, wine isn't a foreign substance."

Only if it comes from France, Italy, or some other wine-producing nation. I motioned to the real James and handed him my cell phone.

"It's your client. She wants to talk to you, Mr. Lessor."

I left the case in his capable hands and walked into our miniscule bathroom to take a hot, cleansing shower.

CHAPTER FIVE

Tentatively, I was on security duty from noon till six so I had the morning free. You never knew, because schedules were always changing. Em's condo was about one hundred yards south of the park where *Deadline Miami* was shooting and the show had actually used a couple of vacant units in her building for interior shots. Em was employed by her contractor father and usually worked from her office at home, so I figured she'd be in when I knocked on her door.

She was.

"Jesus, Skip. I saw *Eye Witness News* this morning. Alison Cole actually mentioned you by name. Said you saw the jump, and she even quoted you. You know, you could have called." She seemed a little put out.

I vaguely remembered mumbling something to a lady with a microphone after we'd talked to the police, but I had no idea what I might have said. I was somewhat in a state of shock.

We walked into her twenty-third-story condo, and as always, I was struck by the view from her floor-to-ceiling glass window.

The marina, the bay, South Beach, and the ocean beyond. In another life, this would be my life.

"How bad was it?"

"We've both seen dead bodies."

"We have," she agreed as she reached up and placed her arm around my neck, pulling me close.

"But to watch someone jump—" there I was, reliving the event— "and fall through the air." I shivered and started to choke. "Then crash to the ground." I couldn't go any further. I had nothing left to relate.

"Celebrities, actors, they're crazy people," she said.

I just nodded.

Em went to the kitchen and came back with two iced teas. We sat on the balcony in cushioned lawn chairs from Front Gate and looked out at the boats on the sparkling water. Serene and peaceful. What had Ashley said about Londell? He was a river of peace? What the hell was that all about?

Composing myself, I said, "I did watch the whole thing. He deliberately jumped, Em. Yet his girlfriend, the lead cop, and James are willing to suspend reality and believe he could have been murdered. I don't get it."

"As close as you are, in the park right next door," she said, staring into my eyes, "you've been a little distant since you and what's-his-name took this security gig. I don't hear from you, see you."

I hadn't seen her every day. The 'gig' as she referred to it required me to work a lot of weird hours, and I was trying to be respectful of her job and personal life. I was never certain that I was the main priority in her life. She was that in my life. No question about it, but I never took Emily for granted.

"As far as me and what's-his-name—" Emily knew James very well, but there was always this friction between the two of them— "it's been a little nuts," I said. "We're dealing with the street crazies, then dealing with the movie crazies."

"The good thing is you're being compensated well. And you could drop by during your free time."

"I'm here now."

I told her about James's side deal with Ashley Amber.

"She's a twit."

One of Em's secret vices was that she read the gossip magazines. *People*, *Us*, even the *National Enquirer* on occasion.

"We've had clients who are twits before."

Sipping her tea, she smiled at me. "Your partner's a twit. Maybe they're suited for each other."

"Should I jump in? Take a cut?"

"You could use the money, boyfriend, but I admire your ethics. If you don't think there's a case, then—"

"But there apparently are some people who do think he was murdered. So maybe there is a case."

Nodding at me she said, "The lady has a lot of jack. She's had a couple of movies in the last year, and now she's on a successful TV series. I'm sure they pay her a boatload of money."

As an actress on *Deadline Miami*, Ashley Amber played a high-priced attorney for a cable news show in The Magic City, and although producer Clint Anders was aiming for a highbrow *West Wing* kind of show, he didn't have any trouble featuring the blonde actress in short skirts, low-cut blouses, and an almost obligatory bikini shot either at her pool or on the beach in every episode. So I kind of likened the program to a *West Wing/ Baywatch* series where Amber played a smart Pam Anderson. But then, this was Ashley Amber so the smart part was a stretch.

"So, do I take the job?"

"Yes."

"Really? You think I should? Even though I am quite certain that this death has an open-and-shut end?"

"Yes."

"You have no problem with this?"

"Skip, you've just told me that Ashley Amber," she rolled her eyes, "the lead detective on the case, your partner, and even the episode director are all wondering if this could have been a murder."

"Yeah, but remember, they're all a little suspect."

Em cocked her head, her eyes wide open.

"Think about what you just said."

"They're all a little suspect?"

"Maybe they are. Maybe one of them *is* a suspect?"

Em always had a unique way of looking at things.

CHAPTER SIX

I am a pragmatist. I approach problems, situations, interests with a realistic viewpoint. I am practical. My father left us when I was young, and I grew up in a loveless home with a mother and sister who fought just to exist. And that is what we did. Exist. Barely. There were never dreams or visions of a grand future. The love of my life, Em, is sometimes even more of a practical person than I am. But James just floats out there on the periphery. That's what drew me to him and why he has been my best friend since childhood. And just when I want to pigeonhole him, when I want to accuse him of being the dreamer I never could be, he surprises me.

"Skip, I want you to be a part of this investigation."

"James, I can't go over this again. You know what I saw and how I feel about the whole thing."

"Amigo, compadre, hear me out."

We sat on the steps of our Airstream aluminum trailer, James drinking a beer and me sipping coffee. He was off today, so he was wearing khaki cargo shorts and a faded T-shirt. I was dressed in a maroon, collared shirt and gray pants, about to report for duty. Security detail had to look presentable.

"Here's where this all comes down."

I couldn't wait to hear the spin.

"You're on a scaffolding seventy feet in the air."

"Okay." To go along with my partner, I pictured myself up there and felt my stomach turn.

"You are going to run maybe twenty feet, look over your shoulder, then leap and position yourself to land on a soft, helium-filled air bag."

"Got it."

"Maybe you're in over your head with personal problems. You're banging the sister of your pregnant wife. Possibly, this has caused you some serious concern. Suicide could be an easy way out."

He was getting it. This was a positive sign.

"Or, maybe that didn't enter the picture." He shifted his perspective. "Look, Skip, there were two grips and a camera guy on that platform. Am I right? Isn't that what you told me?"

"There were. Londell and three others."

"Maybe these guys were contacted by the wife, this Juliana Londell. The lady, this Juliana, she knows he's been having an affair with her sister, and maybe she sees a big insurance claim if he dies."

Randy Roberts had made a point of telling me that the production company had paid a king's ransom to insure Londell for the stunt. So possibly Clint Anders's film company would benefit with the policy. And James was right, if Juliana Londell had taken out a large policy on her husband—

"One of those three guys up there finds a way to trip him. Or distract him. Come on, Skip, that track was narrow. A bump in the road could send him over the edge. It's possible, am I right?"

And I'm sitting there, sober as a church mouse, thinking my

partner, my roommate, was making sense. The entire thing could come down to an insurance claim. But it sure looked like suicide.

"James, I saw what I saw, but—"

"But maybe things were different up top. Up on that catwalk. You were down below, amigo."

"I was." Suddenly this situation was taking on a new dynamic. I was convinced he took a dive. But maybe there were extenuating circumstances.

"Damn it, I'll try."

"Try what?" James had a wry smile on his face, and I knew he was channeling a movie. "Plummeting? I suppose you could try it *once.*"

I knew the quote. It was from *The Muppet Caper*. Said by the famous nasal-sounding actor and singer Kermit the Frog.

"I'll try to believe that murder is a possibility."

"Damn," James said, smiling. "I was ready to take the entire five hundred bucks myself. Now, you're asking for half."

"There's a but."

"*But* what?"

"I'm in for the initial look. That's it. If we see nothing that makes us suspicious, if there is no sign of any foul play, then I take my two fifty and go home. I'm not going to manufacture a scenario where there isn't one, okay?"

He gave me a sideways glance, and I knew I'd tapped into his devious nature. James saw a fat paycheck from a rich movie starlet.

"I'm serious, James. We're not going to make shit up just to string this lady along. Understood?"

"Fine with me, pard. We'll play it straight. And, by the way, who's going to climb the scaffolding tomorrow and check, from seventy feet up, whether there was any glitch in the grid?"

My heart skipped a beat. There was always an ulterior motive with James. I could count on it.

"This is why you're making a case for me to be partner to this? Because you don't want to go up on that catwalk?"

"Hey, I'm going to be interviewing the camera guy and the two grips. They saw the whole thing firsthand."

"James, I can't go up there and—"

"Skip, someone needs to go up there and look around. I am no good with heights. Dude, you know that."

And I remembered a very scary time when I climbed up a very high, teetering carnival ride called The Dragon's Tail to save my partner from a gondola car that was ready to crash to the ground. I'd been scared out of my mind, but I'd done it. Subtly he was reminding me that I had already proven I could do heights. Even if it was to save his worthless ass.

"I don't even think we're allowed up there. There's yellow tape covering the steps and—"

"It's going to take fifteen minutes, Skip. If that. You can pull it off."

"What am I looking for?"

"Come on, Skip, you already have the answer to that question. 'You'll know it when you see it.'"

"Well, I need to do it soon."

"Pard, I'll sub for you on the ground. Right now. All you need is fifteen, twenty minutes tops. You go up on the walkway and see what you can see."

"How many beers have you had?"

"Two."

"It's a good thing you aren't the one going up."

"Son, I've got better balance drunk than most people do sober."

I should have made him prove it.

"James, you said something about the two grips and the camera guy. They were up there watching. There's footage from that camera. I'm certain the cops have already questioned these three, but you really do need to find them and get their recollection. And get a copy of that shoot."

"Like I told you, that's a priority."

"And what about Londell's wife?"

"Born 1989, got a job with William Morris at the tender age of eighteen, DDO Artists Agency a year later, and she quit a year after that to start her own company."

"Ambitious."

"It would seem. Also billed as ruthless."

"Ruthless?"

"Takes what she wants. Doesn't let anyone get in her way. A couple of comments on newsgroups used the words 'ballsy' and 'brassy'. There were some other choice words I won't repeat. For as young as she is, she apparently has taken down some pretty heavy players and," he paused, "she's made some newcomers overnight sensations. Lady doesn't mess around."

And I wondered how some people in their early twenties have the balls to take what they want and make things happen, when some of us are still floundering in our own insecurities.

James took the last swallow of his Yuengling beer, stood up, and walked into the trailer, leaving the door wide open. "I'd better dress a little better since I'm filling in for your security shift," he shouted.

And that meant I was relegated to climbing the scaffolding and walking the catwalk where Jason Londell leaped to his death. What was I even looking for? Maybe I could just check with the cops. Surely they'd canvassed the area. I knew for certain someone had checked out the steel structure, and what would I find that they hadn't? Why should a rookie private investigator go up there, not even sure what he was looking for? I'd take any excuse at all not to make the trip.

"Good luck, amigo. I hope you break open the case."

My heart leaped again and I broke out in a cold sweat.

CHAPTER SEVEN

Part of the makeshift framework was a ladder, allowing the climber access to a walkway twenty-five feet from the ground, and a similar walkway seventy feet from the ground. Seventy feet may not sound that high to you, but think about a friend who is six feet tall. Add another six feet. And another six feet. Another, another, another, another, another, then three more six footers and a couple more feet and you are higher than a kite, my friend. Higher than a frigging kite. James is about six one so I can compare. Me, I'm five ten, five ten and a half on my best days. James is in that elite club. Six foot and over.

I stared up at the tallest part of the metal structure, picturing myself up there, looking down at the catwalk, seeing through the porous grid and wondering how it would feel if I stumbled and fell. I was sick to my stomach.

Yellow vinyl tape ran across the entrance to the structure, warning me this was a crime scene. I didn't really care. I'd been hired to investigate this crime. And if a cop came by and said, "Excuse me, sir, you're not allowed to go up there," I'd push him aside and start climbing.

No, that's not what I would do. I'd actually embrace him, kiss him on the cheek, and say, "Thank you. I didn't want to go up in the first place."

There was no cop. The scene was quiet and filming of the series, which hadn't stopped, had moved to a parking lot across the way. I had no idea what they were doing. Cop cars were in the blacktopped lot, their red-and-blue lights flashing, and I could hear Randy Roberts on a bullhorn, shouting to a handful of extras. Something about making sure they avoided looking at a camera.

I'd never read the script. Had no idea why Jason Londell was supposed to jump. I just knew we were being paid a couple thousand dollars for a week's work, and I didn't want that to go away anytime soon.

I'd changed into jeans and a pair of canvas deck shoes, thinking the rubber soles would give me a better grip on the grid. Again, I was sure the cops had already been up there, and I'm certain they were better equipped to find any clues than I was. So I wondered, what if I just told James that there was nothing new to report? We weren't going to discover new evidence that they had missed. These were trained professionals who investigated crimes for a living on a regular basis. James and me? We'd been lucky in solving a couple of cases. That was it. Trained professionals wasn't exactly an accurate description of *More or Less Investigations*.

With fear, with trepidation, I grasped the sides of the ladder and took that first step. What is it they say about achievement and success? Something about it all starts with the first step. I took that step, doubting I would achieve any success, then another and another, the sun beating down on me and heating the metal ladder. Five feet above the ground and I'm thinking it's a big mistake. Ten feet, I know it is. By the time I reached the twenty-five-foot catwalk, my hands were sweating, perspiration was running into my eyes, and my fingers were wrapped tightly around the warm handrails. If I was smart, I'd go right back down that ladder.

Partnering with James, I'd realized a long time ago I wasn't that smart.

The old adage is, "don't look down." Looking up isn't much better. So I closed my eyes and felt my way up the ladder. When I opened them, I had one more step to go. One more step to seventy feet above the ground.

I was conscious of my heart beating fast and loud. I was short of breath and could feel a tremor in my right hand.

There was a steel bar mounted waist high on the far side of the walkway, and as I took that final wobbly step, I reached out and grabbed it, praying that this whole structure wouldn't come crashing down. I forced myself to look out at the Miami skyline as I fought the overwhelming urge to throw up. Taking a deep breath, loosening my death grip on the steel bar, I glanced down. Big mistake. My brain started swimming and the waves threatened to drown me. I closed my eyes again, trying to gain equilibrium.

Thirty seconds went by and I opened them. I was adjusting, but barely. I focused on the parking lot across the street. Cameras were aimed at a man and woman who appeared to be in a heated argument. The woman in a short, summer dress waved her hand in a dismissive gesture and opened the door of a black Lexus convertible. She started the engine and drove out of the lot. Roberts raised his bullhorn and yelled, "Cut," and all the action ceased. I was certain the actress was Ashley Amber. She seemed to have recovered from her sorrow long enough to go to work.

Holding tightly to the rail, I carefully walked back to where Jason Londell had started his run. The camera guy had been at the far end of the runway, the two grips near him. I was not going to replicate the actor's action. All I had to do was slowly trace his steps, not run them.

The webbed structure lined up east and west so Londell was running west. Straight at the camera. Cautiously I walked the path, staring at the walkway and trying not to look through the grate to the ground seventy feet below. Concentrating on the metal, looking for I didn't know what. Maybe a defect that he tripped over. Maybe something that was lodged in the metal web. Thirty feet of track, and I studied it all. Remains of a trip wire? I saw no sign of that. Then, back again. I took another walk west, feeling a little more comfortable, a little looser, and I gave a glance over my shoulder, just like Londell had done in the first take. But I never, ever, removed my hand from the rail. Not that secure.

The second take was freshest in my mind. Randy Roberts had said, "Action." The cameras had captured the run to make sure the angles were right. I carefully knelt down at the spot where I thought he had jumped. Still reaching up with my left hand and grasping the bar, I ran my right hand over the metal grid. It was smooth. No screw sticking out, no rough metal edges. Standing up, I looked out and noticed the film crew breaking down the scene. I had no idea how Juliana Londell or anyone else could have engineered Jason's death. It was either an accident or suicide. No question.

I walked to the far end where the cameraman had been. It was a handheld so there were no mounts. Two grips, the camera guy, and Jason Londell. Three of them came back down the ladder. One of them took the express route. My final act was to look almost straight down where the now deflated air bag sprawled on the green park grass. I tried to picture myself jumping on that bag and immediately felt my stomach clench. I remembered Roberts's first words to me.

"Sometimes it's just stupid to do your own stunts."

I had to agree.

Rubbing my rubber-soled shoes over the webbed surface of the walkway, I checked for any moisture. Maybe the scaffold had been a little slippery, and he'd slid as he was running. Everything seemed to be dry.

With a final visual sweep of the walkway, I eased myself down the ladder very slowly. When I came off the last step, I thought about kissing the earth. I may have done it, but a voice behind stopped me cold.

"What were you doing up there, kid?"

I turned around and an older guy, about forty-five, stood there, arms crossed, frowning at me.

"I was just—" I froze.

"Give me an answer."

His salt-and-pepper hair was combed back in a rather severe style, his gray trousers creased razor sharp. Even in this heat, he wore a sport coat, and the shine on his shoes could have blinded someone. I stared at his eyes, but they were hidden behind a pair of Ray-Ban aviators.

"Who wants to know?"

"Kid, I do. Either you tell me what the hell you were doing on that walk up there, or I'll have security get involved. Understood?"

I knew security. Hell, I was security.

"There's a good explanation why I was up there, and I'll be happy to tell you if you tell me who you are."

I am usually not the person who pushes back, but this pompous guy was getting on my nerves. And, besides that, I shouldn't have been up there and I knew it. Anyway, what business was it of his?

"Do you know who you're talking to?"

"Obviously not."

"I'm Clint Anders. I own this dog-and-pony show. I produce

Deadline Miami and I will not have some upstart punk tell me—"

"Ahhh, Mr. Anders."

Goodbye paycheck. Goodbye job.

"I'm so sorry. I'm with the security team on this set, and I was up there—" I stumbled, searching for a reason why I was up there. And then it hit me. I didn't have to make up a story.

"I was up there trying to figure out if something on the grid caused Jason Londell to fall. Just following up, sir."

He stood there for a moment, arms still crossed. Finally, he took off the glasses and nodded his head. Reaching inside his jacket pocket, Anders pulled out a packet of cigarettes, lighting one with a gold lighter.

"Cops were already there." He took a deep drag, slowly exhaling, and watching me with a sly look.

"Yes, sir, but I just wanted to cover the bases. I took it upon myself to—"

"You took it upon yourself?"

I nodded.

"I actually admire people who take some initiative."

I let out a breath.

He turned and walked away. After three steps, he stopped and looked over his shoulder, just like Londell was supposed to do.

"Kid, don't do it again. You hear me?"

I didn't have to be told twice.

CHAPTER EIGHT

"Nothing's up there, James."

We'd settled in for a glass of wine at Em's condo. It was five o'clock, and we watched a cruise ship docking at the causeway, half a mile away. The view was breathtaking from her balcony.

"Well, it was a shot." He sipped his deep-red beverage, his feet propped on an expensive white wicker stool. "I did a little digging on this Juliana Londell. She is pregnant. Apparently, about three months along. Has only been married to Londell for a year. She met him at a party, he hired her as his agent, whirlwind romance, then he left her. When they broke up, he fired her."

"They're still married?" Em asked.

"I couldn't see where they'd filed for divorce."

"And now Londell is banging her sister."

"*Was* banging her sister. But it's Hollywood, Em. Movie stars. When you wish upon a star and all that."

She gave him a sly look. "It happens in Miami too, James."

"Yeah, but these Hollywood types. They're a little different."

"So," Em said, "she's jealous? That's why she bumped him off? Or does she collect a big insurance settlement if he dies?"

The insurance thing again.

"Here's the thing," James said. "I want to find out if she's in California. If she's still on the West Coast, then she hired someone here to—" He stopped, not sure where to go with his statement.

"Exactly," I stated the obvious. "To *what*? There's nothing up on that scaffold, and believe me, I looked very hard. No sign anyone was murdered."

"Boys, you've got video, don't you? Skip, you said that they filmed the second run-up there on the scaffolding."

As usual, she got to the heart of the matter. Ashley Amber's five hundred bucks bought her my trip up the seventy-foot-high whatever it was, and it should have bought a review of the footage from two cameras. Another reason I was glad Em was on the case. Excellent point.

I looked at James. "Weren't you supposed to interview the camera guy and grips? You were going to get some copies of the shoot."

"I was filling in for your shift, amigo. Not much time. So where do we get the video?" James finished his wine, stretching and getting up. I knew he was headed to the refrigerator for a beer.

"From the two camera guys, James. The ones you have yet to talk to. Remember? The two guys who you were going to interview."

"Settle down, amigo," he yelled from inside. "You know these guys, am I right?"

"As a matter of fact, I do," I answered. "One of them. I talked to the guy on the ground the other day about his camera."

James returned with two beers. Beers I'd bought and paid for, because Em doesn't have beer in her refrigerator. He handed me one, top already popped.

"Thanks for the wine, Em, but it's not my favorite beverage." He gave her a patronizing smile.

"*Deadline Miami* shoots in three perf thirty-five millimeter, so the show is all on film."

He took a swallow of his Yuengling and rolled his eyes at me.

"Three perf what?"

"It's the same film stock as four perf, but it costs a lot less with three perforations."

"Why is this important to us?"

"The perforations are what pull the film through the camera. And I assume, through the projector."

"Jeez, why don't they just go digital?"

"Hey, I only talked to the guy for about ten minutes. I'm not an expert. He did say that film gave the project a much cleaner look, but Clint Anders, the hotshot producer I met, had decided that starting next episode, he was going to go to digital, even though it wouldn't be as crisp."

"Why would you reduce the quality of the show?" Em asked.

"I guess all the shows are starting to go digital, but my camera guy said Anders is doing it for economic reasons, too. The production was having some problems. Going over budget, technical problems, inflated salaries, and then, I suppose, this Londell thing won't help. Basically, you can save a lot of money if you go to sixteen millimeter and even more if you shoot digital. So he's cutting costs."

"Mm," James thought about it. "Film just sounds so old-school. I didn't think anyone used film anymore."

"*Two and a Half Men, Castle, Grey's Anatomy*, according to this guy, a lot of shows he's worked for in the past have been filmed in thirty-five mil."

"Okay. Who is this guy?"

"Guy's name is Jerry Clemens. He gave me a card." I opened my wallet and found it immediately.

"Card? Old-school, my friend. Put the information in your phone."

I dialed the number, and he picked up on the first ring.

"Jerry, this is Skip Moore. You and I talked several days ago about your camera and how they shot the episode."

"Hey, I remember. Man, I saw you there yesterday when that whole thing went down. Totally unbelievable."

"I was wondering. This isn't from head of security or any-thing, but I wondered if I could get like a digital print on the two camera angles. The one from the top and yours. Just to review."

"I ran a digital copy for the cops. Sent 'em an attachment. I can send you the same thing."

"Man, that would be great. What about the shot from seventy feet up?"

"Funny thing about that."

"Yeah?"

"Guy was a sub. They hired him through a temp agency. He'd never worked the show before. Disappeared after the accident, and no one has seen him since."

"That's a little strange."

"I think he freaked out. He'll probably show later, all shook up."

"So, the footage is where?"

"It was a handheld. Aaton Penelope thirty-five-millimeter camera. Pretty good piece. Apparently, he took it with him."

"Wow. No one stopped him, no one saw—"

"Hey, Moore, it was chaos down there. Remember? Were you looking for a runaway cameraman? I know I wasn't. I mean, we had a dead celebrity to contend with. Am I right?"

"The cops are looking for him?"

"All I know is, I told them the same story. I know the agency where they hired him. I use 'em sometimes to get work."

"Who is it?"

"Howell Video and Sound. Run by a guy named Scott Howell. Now there's a guy who knows his way around cameras."

"Got his number?"

"Sure."

He gave it to me, and I repeated it as my technical assistant, James, punched it into his phone.

"Hey, Jerry, thanks for everything." I gave him my e-mail address, and he promised to send the video in the next few minutes.

"You want to explain the other half of that conversation? Should have put him on speaker," James said.

"The camera guy on the grid? He was a temp. By the time the dust settled, he'd disappeared. No one has seen him or his camera since."

"Skip," Em stood and put her hand on my arm. I looked into her beautiful face, framed by her long blonde hair, and for a moment forgot that James was on the same balcony. "I think you have probable cause to take the case and bill this girl, Ashley Amber. Your partner is right. I've got a feeling there's more to Jason Londell's death than a jump off the scaffolding."

CHAPTER NINE

Ten minutes later the e-mail arrived. Eagerly, Em opened the video and expanded it to full screen.

There was no sound. Nothing had been miked. All sound effects would have been added later. And the camera was stable, a fixed focus, as it was mounted and there was no movement. The handheld camera upstairs was to be more fluid, to give the leap more urgency.

"Was this a death jump?"

Em raised her eyebrows. "What?"

"No, no. Did the *show* call for him to die? Was it in the script?"

"You know," I looked at James, "I really never read the script. I have no clue. Did you?"

"No, but he was only in this episode. And they're still filming, so it could have been his last scene. God, I hope they don't use the real splat scene in the show."

"That's not going to happen, James," Emily recoiled. "Sometimes you can be so gross."

If it was the last scene, they could show the jump, then move on. With Londell's death, ratings would be through the roof. Maybe the entire show could be revived from an almost certain cancellation at the end of the year. But then they seldom shoot scenes in order, so there was a strong possibility that they didn't have all of Jason Londell's shots in the can and they might have to scrap his part in the show and recast.

"Let's see what's on the film." I held my breath, not wanting to relive the episode.

Ground camera, as it was called, started a few seconds before Randy Roberts said action. Jason Londell stood still for maybe two seconds, then started running the grid. Three seconds into the run, he leaped, and I watched in horror as he plummeted toward the ground. The camera never picked up the final crash as the trajectory should have been to the inflated air bag. The falling body disappeared in the shot maybe ten feet before he would have landed. Thank God, we didn't have to see it.

"That's it?" James seemed disappointed.

"You wanted to see the body explode on the ground?"

"No. I expected something to happen on the walkway."

"I told you—"

"Run it again."

Em hit replay, and we watched the same scene. Again and again and again. There seemed to be nothing left to see.

"Can we stop it at any point?" James asked.

"Sure," Em started it again, hitting the stop button, freezing Londell in mid-stride. "Just tell me where."

"A tenth of a second before he jumps."

She didn't get it exactly, but we watched, anticipating the leap.

"Stop it."

She did.

"Right there. Watch his reaction. Run it again and let it go."

She played the short scene again, and I concentrated. A tenth of a second before he jumped I saw it too. A slight jerk of his body. His head went up, he seemed to tense up, but, then again, it was probably in anticipation of his final fall.

"I don't think you've got anything, James. It was probably a natural reaction." I was as disappointed as he was.

"We've got a cameraman who disappeared along with his film. That's a start, don't you think?"

Em had agreed. It was probably enough to take the investigation a step further.

"How are we going to handle this?" I asked.

"I'd suggest five hundred a day plus expenses. One of you may have to fly out to L.A. And I might have to go along to assist," she said, smiling at me.

"Five hundred dollars a day. Not bad. We give it two weeks and see if we can find this camera guy and locate Londell's wife. We check to see if she'd taken out a big insurance claim recently, see if Juliana Londell is on the up-and-up, and we make ourselves—" James was already computing.

"Seven thousand dollars," Em said.

I was a business major in school, but Em was a math genius. She could do major computations in her head.

"Split three ways, that's two thousand three hundred thirty-three dollars apiece."

"Split three ways? Apiece? You're suggesting—" James squinted his eyes, looking at her suspiciously.

"Have you solved any of your cases without my help?"

She stood there, hands on her beautiful hips, waiting for his answer.

"Well, have you?"

"Have you ever butted out?" he asked.

"Come on, James. I've brought you guys more cases than you've found on your own. And in this case, the Jason Londell murder, I've already helped you."

As he started to interrupt, she held up her hand.

"And I'm not taking any part of your five-hundred-dollar retainer. I'm not asking for any of Ashley Amber's first check. That's the kind of partner I am."

Em didn't need the money. I was convinced of that. Her father paid her very well, but the truth was, the three of us did work well together, and she usually came up with ideas we never would have considered. And, if she was going to participate, she wanted to be compensated.

James looked at me, a dejected, hangdog look on his face. I shrugged my shoulders. If we had any chance of solving this case for Amber Ashley, Em would be a huge asset. James knew it, I knew it, and Em definitely knew it. She really did have a high opinion of herself.

My girlfriend stood, picked up the wine glasses and empty beer bottles, and walked to the kitchen.

"Guys, I suggest we call Amber right now. Tell her what we know. Make the pitch and get her reaction. Then Skip finds an after-hours number for this Scott Howell. If we wait until tomorrow morning to talk to the temp agency, our cameraman will be that much farther ahead of us." Tossing the bottles into her recycle bin and placing the wine glasses in the porcelain sink, she turned to James.

"James, I think you should finish your research on Jason Londell's wife, and we probably should run a background on our client. She was screwing her sister's husband, so I'm guessing she's got some kind of history."

James frowned. "And if we're splitting this three ways, what are you going to be doing?"

"Besides organizing this operation? I'm going to talk with Jason Londell's good friend, Clint Anders. He hired Londell, they've known each other forever, and there's probably a lot of light he could shed on the matter."

James shook his head in amazement.

"You think you've got this thing all under control, don't you?"

"James," she gave him her three-carat dazzling white-teeth smile, "I don't *think* so. I know so. You know it too. These things have to be done. I'm just organizing them for you."

Nodding, he headed toward the door.

"Two thousand plus bucks for two weeks' work. It's a whole lot more than I make at my real job."

The door shut behind him, and as we stood there, Em grabbed my hand.

"Did I get a little too full of myself?"

"You?"

"Come on, I was trying to goad him a little. I shouldn't have."

"The day you two get along, I'm going to be very worried."

"I'm right, aren't I? We've got to cover all bases."

"You're right."

"Then let's find this Scott Howell. He placed the temp cameraman and that could be the key to this whole thing."

CHAPTER TEN

Ashley Amber said yes so fast, I wish we'd asked for more money. She asked when James and I could start, and I told her we were already on the clock. Another thousand down and everything was good to go.

She asked for periodic updates and wanted to know if we were including a trip to California. I told her we were just formulating our plan, and she thanked me for everything. I made no promises, but told her we had a couple of leads already.

Howell Video and Sound was open when I called. "Till eight," the clerk announced. The building was on Northeast 4th Court, a couple blocks off Biscayne Boulevard. The area was industrial, with railroad tracks running behind the studio/equipment rental building. Scraggly live oaks and scrub brush grew on the sides of the road and pushed themselves onto a cracked, concrete sidewalk running along the far side of the street. We drove by long, low warehouses with front loaders and cargo haulers in neat rows out front. Miller's Commercial Dry Cleaning, Eagle Logistics, and Marve's Auto Body Repair Shop rounded out the block.

Em drove her new Mercedes SL500 with retractable hardtop. Probably not the car to navigate this neighborhood, but Em had no fear. She never has had. As long as I've known her.

We pulled into the parking lot next to a Chevy pickup towing an enclosed trailer.

Howell Video and Sound
Grip Trailer

was stenciled on the side.

Pushing open the glass door, I was immediately surrounded by small cranes, dollies, dedolights, hanging klieg lights, follow spots, and more. Two weeks ago I would have had no idea what they were. Less than a week on the set, I had a passing knowledge.

Standing behind a counter on the far side of the spacious room was a young man on his cell phone. As we approached, he hung up and smiled at us.

"If you don't see it here," he waved his hand at the inventory, "we've got a pretty big warehouse out back. What can I do for you?"

"We're looking for Scott Howell."

"You guys in the business?"

Actually, I was. In the movie business. Just as I was in the security business when Clint Anders asked me what I was doing on his scaffolding. A chameleon. Blending in wherever I could.

"That's us."

"I'll see if Scott is free. You're lucky he's in. Guy is always flying somewhere. Japan, Austria, London, New York." He picked up a landline and dialed an extension. Speaking softly into the receiver, he listened to the answer. Turning to us, he said, "He'll be right out."

The Howell guy was around forty-five, dressed in jeans and a collared shirt, a three-day growth of sandy-brown stubble on his face, and a pair of Oakley sunglasses pushed up on his head.

"Let me guess. You two are getting ready to film the surprise hit of next summer and you need not only some top-notch equipment, but expert advice. Am I close?"

Em smiled, her eyes meeting his. "The advice maybe."

"So I'm not making any money on this transaction? Well, at least I've gotten to meet you."

I bristled. He was flirting with my girlfriend like I wasn't in the room. I got that a lot. I hadn't gotten used to it, but I got it a lot.

"Mr. Howell, I'm certain the police have already come to you," I said, "but we're here to find out who the cameraman was on the *Deadline Miami* shoot when Jason Londell fell from the scaffolding."

"Ah, jeez, I couldn't believe that. What a tragedy. So, you guys aren't with the cops?"

"No," Em shook her head. "We're with a private investigation firm, and we've been hired to investigate the fall."

Investigation firm. All of a sudden I felt kind of grown-up. We weren't just two P.I.s who stumbled through some cases, we were now an investigation firm. Leave it Em to bring a degree of professionalism to the job.

"Cops haven't been here. Why would they?"

"The production company hired a camera operator who came from Howell Video and Sound along with a camera, am I right?"

"The company rented a camera. What are you asking about the operator? I don't think we had anything to do with the operator."

I seriously believed the guy had no clue.

"Scott," Em was getting a little more personal, "does this cameraman, does he do a lot of work for you?"

"Like I said, I don't think we had anything to do with the guy. But I didn't make the deal. Hold on a minute, let me see what I can find."

Walking over to the counter, Howell started working a laptop computer, keying in code words, and bringing information up on the screen.

"Greg Handler was the operator. Man didn't work for us. In fact, I have no idea who this guy is."

"Oh. One of our operators, Jerry Clemens, said the production hired him through your company."

"No. Somebody got the wrong information. Greg Handler came in here and rented a camera. There was a letter of authorization from somebody associated with the show. He said he was on temporary assignment and he'd need it for a week. I'd never seen the guy before."

"You checked with the production company?"

"I'm sure we did. Guy paid rental in advance plus insurance. Let's see," he scanned the screen. "Company credit card. CA Productions."

Clint Anders.

"How much is rental?"

"This cam? Fifteen hundred."

"For five days," Em asked. "Wow."

"Per day. Fifteen hundred per day. Plus, fifteen hundred insurance."

"Nine thousand, up front?" She seemed surprised. I knew I was.

"That's one reason productions are so expensive these days. But," he added, "he didn't have to buy it or maintain it. That's where it gets really expensive."

"You never heard of this guy before?"

"We know most of the locals. Jerry Clemens has worked out of here before, but this guy apparently came in from L.A."

Em looked at me. "Company credit card."

We'd have to track that down.

"Hey, why all the questions? And you mentioned cops."

"Scott, Mr. Howell, this Greg Handler, did he give you any I.D.?"

"Driver's license. Why the questions?"

"Do you have a copy?"

Keying in a few more letters, he turned the screen toward us, and there was Greg Handler's California license photo, with dark hair over his ears, a Tom Selleck bushy mustache, and a rather large nose. Not just long, but bulbous. He looked like someone right out of central casting. To top it all off, he had on a pair of tinted glasses. Not sunglasses, but tinted like they were custom made. But they hid his eyes very well. Prescription probably.

"One more time, kids, what's with all the questions?" Scott Howell sounded somewhat irritated.

"He's got what? Two more days on the rental?"

"Two."

"Maybe there's nothing to worry about."

"And why should I consider worrying?"

"Because he disappeared after Londell died." Em broke the bad news.

"Disappeared." He said it as a statement, not a question.

"Disappeared." I echoed his word.

"Hasn't been heard from since," Em said.

There was a moment of awkward silence.

"My camera?"

"Maybe it will turn up at the end of the rental period," Em said.

"Maybe it won't," I countered. "The camera and a film of that final leap are missing along with Mr. Handler."

"When I first saw you," he nodded to Emily, "I thought this was going to be a good day. A very good-looking lady walks into my business, things brighten up. And now you bring me this."

"I learned something a long time ago, Scott." Emily had a

cynical smile on her face. "And you being in the film business, you should have learned it too."

"What's that?"

I waited for the drumroll.

"Looks can be deceiving."

Bada boom.

CHAPTER ELEVEN

"There's got to be a reason the cops haven't called on this Howell guy. Jerry Clemens turned his shoot over to the cops. They know there'd been another shoot. They've got to be looking for the other camera."

Em nodded as she drove. "I'm sure they are. And assuming Howell is telling us the truth, they'll have the same obstacle that we have."

Maybe, just maybe, we were thinking faster than the cops. Howell had to be on their radar.

"The guy looked weird."

"Scott Howell? I thought he was very attractive. I could go for a guy like that. Very Hollywood."

"No," I snapped. "Not Howell. Greg Handler. Weird."

"Well, he's a different Hollywood."

"There's that."

Without warning, Em wheeled into a 7-Eleven, pulled between the parking lines, and stopped the car. Reaching into her purse, she pulled out her iPhone.

"Greg Handler," she said. "I'm going to Google him. What do I put in? Camera guy? Cinematographer?"

"Both."

She keyed in something and stared at the tiny screen.

"Nothing. Doesn't recognize the name."

"I would guess that *Deadline Miami* is a union production. I'm certain that CA Productions is union. I don't see how you could work in Hollywood if you weren't. See what organization he and Jerry would belong to."

In seconds she had it. "American Cinematographers Association. ACA."

"So Google search ACA with Handler's name."

She did.

"Here he is. Name: Greg Handler. Cinematographer. Location: Los Angeles, California. Member since 1999."

"Any other background?"

"Wow," she said. "Loads of movies. *Casino Royale, Borat.*"

"His picture looked like Borat with that bushy mustache."

"*Hope Springs, The Devil Wears Prada*, and what does DP mean?"

"Director of Photography. He supervises the other camera guys."

"Or camera girls."

"Yeah. And every hot girl who can aim a camera thinks she's a photographer. Ooh, look at me, I took a picture of a lawn chair and it's all shadowy."

"What is that all about?" she asked.

"Never mind, it's just a quote from that cartoon character, Stewie, on *Family Guy*."

"Are you ever going to grow up?"

"What were you watching a couple of weeks ago when I visited you? *Jersey Shore*?"

Em pouted. "Okay, point taken."

"Why the question about DP?"

"Well, Handler was DP on a couple of TV series. *Scrubs, How I Met Your Mother*, so I guess his qualifications are pretty good."

"So why did he split?" I asked. "He shoots the jump, then disappears. It doesn't make any sense. Especially since he's got a really stellar track record."

We sat in the car, both of us wondering where Greg Handler had disappeared to. Wondering what had happened on that catwalk.

"I'll do some looking when we get back," Em said, still staring out the windshield. "If he's listed on the union page, I should be able to contact him through there."

"Good idea." And then I remembered. "Randy told me his agent got him this gig. So maybe you have to go through an agent. That's great if the agent knows where Handler is, but if he got him this gig and then loses touch for a while it may be difficult to run him down."

"We'll see when I get back."

She started the car and the quiet purr of the engine reminded me this wasn't my in-the-shop 2003 Chevy. This was a refined machine, and driving it was a, for the most part, refined woman. Except when she wasn't.

"Was there a photo on that union page?"

"No. I looked," she said. "You know how they use a blank silhouette if someone doesn't post a photo on Facebook?"

"Yeah."

"That's what it was. Blank."

"Well, if we run into him, I think I'd recognize him."

"Distinctive."

She drove me to the set, and I met James at the trailer.

"Late shoot tonight, pard. We've got to be on duty at eight. It may last until midnight."

As we walked, I talked him through the afternoon's activities, and he told me about his day's work.

"The key grip was up there. Chad somebody, I've got it written down. Anyway, this guy met the cameraman. You said Greg Handler? Chad says the guy was pleasant and told him that he'd worked this kind of shot before. Filming a fall. Very confident. Chad and his assistant were a yard or so back from the camera when Londell jumped, fell, whatever he did. He told me that they were shocked still for about three or four seconds, then scrambled down the ladder as fast as they could. They never paid any attention to this camera guy and forgot him in all the commotion."

I tossed a photocopy of Greg Handler's driver's license onto the small kitchen table. James glanced at it.

"James, I have to admit it all sounds strange." I pointed to the piece of paper.

"What's that?"

"We had Howell make us a copy of the guy's California license so we'd recognize him if we ever ran into him."

"This is Greg Handler?" James picked up the paper, studied it for a second, and shook his head.

"That's the guy. I told Em he looks like Sacha Baron Cohen in *Borat*."

"Chad, my grip, he said the guy was slender, blond, and about thirty-five. Good looking, well spoken—"

"We're talking the camera guy on the scaffolding?"

"The same."

"Only different," I said. "This guy is not blond, not slender, and he passed thirty-five ten years ago."

CHAPTER TWELVE

Clint Anders was on the set. Second time I'd laid eyes on him. According to Bill Purdue, our head of security, Anders hadn't been seen in three weeks. The show seemed to survive without his daily presence.

This time he had his arm around Ashley Amber, brushing her hair with his free hand, and talking to her in a quiet voice. They walked by me on the set and neither one seemed to notice. They appeared to be lost in one another.

Anders had come in the day before Londell died to do some technical advising, and was to fly back to L.A. today. The advising sounded like a tax write-off to me, an excuse to see his friend Londell, but I only know what I learned in business school. James and I had never had to worry about tax write-offs.

We'd heard that Anders was staying in Miami a couple of days while the coroner's office dealt with the body. When they released it, he was going to fly back to Los Angeles for the funeral. I wondered if consoling Ashley was part of his plan. They seemed very cozy.

As I approached James, he gave me a short wave and started in immediately.

"Problem is," he said as he stood on the sidewalk by the street, making sure no one got onto the grassy area where filming was about to begin, "Ashley was apparently right. They found a foreign substance in Londell's body. A foreign substance."

"What is it?"

"No one is saying, but it seems pretty serious."

"So he was high on drugs?"

"Could be."

"Unless this wife, Juliana, personally injected a needle into his arm, I don't see any guilt," I said.

"They found something, partner."

"How do you know?"

"The buzz. Over in the dinner tent. About an hour ago when I grabbed a sandwich people were talking. I mean everyone."

"And rumor becomes fact?"

"Remember, Ashley said she had it on good authority."

"Ashley Amber doesn't seem to be the most reliable person out there, you know?"

"People seem pretty sure, partner."

I just shook my head. If Londell was high on something and sailed off that scaffolding assuming he could fly, then the murder theory flew away with him. We were desperate for facts, but instead, were ingesting rumors and half-truths. None of it was helping us get any further with the case.

"Em's working the other end, right?" James asked.

She was. We'd made a decision that since James and I were being paid by the Anders organization as security, we couldn't let him know we were moonlighting on his set. It was almost like double-dipping, trying to prove Jason Londell's death was not suicide. So Em was going to interview Clint Anders tonight. Em wasn't on anyone's payroll so she was safe. She'd tell him she was a part-time investigator and ask him about his relationship with Londell. From what we could find on the Internet and through conversation with some of the crew, Anders and Londell were good friends and had worked a number of projects on the West Coast. We assumed he knew Londell's wife, Juliana, and Em was going to go for details on her. She'd get what she could and report back to us. She was also going to see how a cameraman that no one seemed to know had access to a CA credit card.

Behind us, about twenty yards, bright lights beamed through the dark of night, and extras in formal suits, black tuxedos, and brightly colored ball gowns were walking down a staged white staircase that pretended to empty into a fancy outdoor cocktail party, complete with champagne glasses, a full-service bar, and white-jacketed waiters offering hors d'oeuvres. It was the kind of party that James, with his culinary degree, would probably want to cater.

"Action," I heard Randy Roberts shout through his bullhorn as the scene began. "Slower. Take your time, stretch it."

I could see him in his canvas director's chair, holding his signature aluminum coffee mug and I was half tempted to ask him if I could have a sip of whatever he was mixing in there, but security can't drink on the job. Apparently, a director can and did drink all day long.

After several retakes he yelled, "Cut," and things came to a halt.

When the lights were switched off, James and I took our scheduled break as Roberts shouted, "Fifteen minutes, people."

"Hey, pard, there's Chad. Let me grab him for a brief chat."

A minute later the tall, lanky black man walked over and shook my hand. He was fairly young, but was going bald and compensated with a mustache and goatee.

Chad Rich had been a grip for ten years. He'd started working in Hollywood on the TV show *Vegas*. He told me it wasn't that easy to get work in this business.

"Man, we're scrambling for jobs. Always. You find a good vehicle, you stick with it. Reality shows are sucking up the money. If it's not a reality show, it's sports networks and movie networks. Shows like *Deadline Miami* are scarce, man, and I am lucky to be where I am."

Chad Rich, James, and I were sitting at a picnic table outside a long gunmetal gray trailer. This trailer housed five members of the crew. I don't know how long it was, but it contained five small housing units lined up next to each other. They were for the grips, scenery, prop, camera people. The actors had a bigger trailer, and the four stars of the show had monster trailers all to themselves. Of course, James and I had a rundown Airstream that had seen much better days. The pecking order was everything.

Everyone except for a couple of security guys was on this short break, and I was enjoying the cool evening breeze and the laid-back Miami park atmosphere. The grassy area was on the water, and I could smell the salty air and the odor of iodine and rotting seaweed. Not that unpleasant, but I guess you would have to be here and breathe it in yourself to understand.

"I know James talked to you," I said, nodding to my partner, "but we've come up with some other questions. Thoughts about Greg Handler. He was the camera guy up on the scaffolding, right?"

I handed him the copy of the driver's license.

"James says he doesn't think this is the Handler you saw."

"No, man." He studied the photo. "Not even close. This guy looks like makeup did a bad job on him. Is that his real stash?"

"Couldn't be a picture from a long time ago?" I wanted to make sure. "Maybe four or five years ago?"

"No way," he said.

"This guy," James was explaining, "supposedly rented a camera from Howell Video and Sound. With a company credit card."

"The guy in the photograph?"

"The same. Gave his name as Greg Handler. Said he was filling in on *DM* and paid in advance for the rental and the insurance." James folded his hands in front of him. I wondered if we were giving this guy too much information.

"Scott Howell, he met with him?"

"No. One of Howell's employees. You know Scott Howell?" James asked.

"Lot of people in this industry know him. Big-time camera guy. Invented some gear that would blow your mind. I actually did meet him on a set in New York with the Rolling Stones."

"Anyway, you're telling us there is no way the Greg Handler in this picture is the Greg Handler you met on that structure?" I pointed at the scaffolding that was still in place, towering over the set.

"Guys, it isn't the same person. My Greg was a blond, short hair, and wore a big thick black leather bracelet. He was like thirty something. The guy in this picture is an aging hippy. And I'm too young to even know what a hippy was."

"Can you explain it?" I asked.

"No."

"Okay," James said. "We're just trying to get all the information we can."

"Are you cops? You can tell me, man. I'm just wondering why the big press for details?"

"You haven't heard from the cops?"

"Except for that short interview, no."

"Well, I would bet that you will. In the very near future." I smiled. So again we were ahead of the organized law enforcement agency? Maybe we really did have a clue as to what we were doing. We at least had an idea. Or maybe we were way off base.

CHAPTER THIRTEEN

James headed back to the Airstream, and I strolled over to the scaffold. Standing about where Londell had landed, I gazed up, finding the fateful launchpad. I closed my eyes for just a moment and pictured the video we'd seen. The run, the slight hesitation or jerk of the body, then the fall from seventy feet up until he was out of the frame. I'd seen the real jump, and Londell never went out of frame in that version. I felt an involuntary shudder.

Dim security lights threw faint shadows on the ground, and the monolithic structure with its puzzle pattern laid ghostly images on the grass, almost like a maze where a rat has to find a piece of cheese.

I still had no idea what the scene they were filming entailed. And why did they need the steel configuration? Walking under the catwalk and gazing up seventy feet above my head, I wondered what was going through the mind of the three crew members moments before Londell went airborne.

Did they have a clue? Did they see a look on his face that would have told them he had lost it? Or were they all blindsided by the disaster? Or could one of them have been responsible for the jump? Responsible for his death. Did someone say something to him? Did they set up a trip wire? There was still that idea. Or maybe all three were in on this together. Dozens of ideas flooded my mind as I stood on the ground looking up.

The phony camera guy, Greg Handler; Chad Rich, the grip; and—I had no idea who the third person was. No frigging idea. Another stellar investigating job by *More or Less Investigations*. Sometimes we really missed the obvious. No one knew who the third guy was. I had to lay this one on James, but then, I always lay the blame on Lessor. And I'm almost always right.

When the breeze died down, the warm, still evening was almost cloying. The humidity coming off the bay and the eighty-plus-degree temperature covered me in a damp coating of moisture. As I turned, ready to walk back to the trailer, I heard what sounded like a cough or someone clearing their throat. Very soft.

Maybe a tropical bird. Maybe a motorboat starting up on the bay. Then faintly another cough, on the backside of the scaffold. Now stone-cold silence. Was someone out there watching me? Or just innocently having a cigarette break? I sniffed the air. No sign of tobacco.

"Is somebody there?"

No response.

"Hello?"

Nothing.

I considered walking toward the sound, making loud sounds like clearing my throat and stomping on the ground as I walked. I had several options, but I also possess the courage of the Tin Man. No courage at all. So I stood still for several minutes, then crept back to our trailer.

I was convinced someone had been following me, watching me. I just didn't have the courage to find out who it was. And then I was confused. Maybe it was the lion who wanted courage. The Tin Man wanted the heart. I figured James would remember so I didn't worry about it.

CHAPTER FOURTEEN

At midnight we met Em at Primos, a trendy club in the lobby of her condo building. Crowded around a small table, I watched the bar as leggy European women in short skirts, young men with airbrushed tans, and guys and girls in jeans and T-shirts all jock-eyed for position, ordering outrageously priced drinks with infused vodka or spiced rum.

"Greg Handler is not Greg Handler," I said.

"Is this a riddle?" she asked.

"No. The photograph doesn't match the description that the crew recalls. Our picture doesn't even come close."

"Then who is he? The guy we have in the driver's license photo?"

"The guy who is the head grip says the photo doesn't look anything like the camera guy he met."

"Makes no sense."

"Chad, the grip, says our photo looks like a bad makeup job."

Em smiled and rolled her eyes.

"We're in the middle of make-believe, boys. Movie magic.

Someone could make up anyone to look different. We women do it all the time."

"And, someone can fake a driver's license. This entire business revolves around fooling one hundred percent of the people." I realized Em was right. We were in the middle of make-believe.

"And," Em added, "so far someone seems to be doing a pretty good job of fooling everyone."

"You talked to Clint Anders?" James wanted to make sure she was earning her third of the take.

"I did, James. He was reluctant at first, but I told him I'd been hired by a third party and that I was harmless. I explained I just wanted some general information, so he agreed. The guy seemed genuinely broken up about the suicide. The death."

Looking at me, James said, "There's a lot of money riding on this, amigo. You know if it was suicide, we don't have a case."

"Well," Em stated, "Clint thinks the man took his own life. When I talked to him, there was no question about it."

"He was a good friend. Any reasons?"

"His marriage was over. He was distraught."

"Distraught?" James frowned. "Over a failed Hollywood marriage? Man, if everyone out there who got divorced decided to off themselves, there wouldn't be any movie actors left. Look, he was murdered."

"Okay," I agreed, "let's assume he was murdered. After all, we're collecting a nice paycheck from Ashley Amber to prove that's the case. Anders flew in the day before the death—before the murder. Strange timing, since he hasn't been here in three weeks, don't you think?"

"He had to show up sometime. After all, it is his show." Now Em was sticking up for him. "He was grateful Londell had agreed to do the guest shot. He thought it would boost ratings and he wanted to be here to thank Londell personally." She folded her hands and was silent for a moment. "I felt bad for him, Skip. The guy is taking it personally. He must have said it three times. If he hadn't invited him out to do the guest spot, Londell would be alive right now."

Hard to dispute.

"He and Londell spent some time together the night before, and he said they talked about coming up through the ranks. It all sounded pretty heartfelt."

"And I heard the time spent together was playing poker with Randy Roberts and a couple of high rollers from South Beach," James said. "Apparently, our Mr. Anders and Londell play for serious money. Rumored to be one reason Mr. Anders is having a little financial trouble."

I'd heard rumors about games on the set too, but James and I could barely afford to play for pennies. We weren't likely to be asked to sit in.

"Em, Greg Handler, or whoever the camera guy really is, used a company credit card to rent and insure the camera. Company credit card. How did Anders explain that? Or did he?" I asked.

"Stolen."

"Convenient."

"While I interviewed him, he called some finance lady. She apparently approves expenses. She told Anders that they did in fact hire an extra cameraman, and poker player Randy Roberts, the director whom you were next to when Londell died, was responsible for making it all happen. Apparently, Roberts thought everything was on the up-and-up and didn't worry about it."

"What? That sounds very convoluted. Who put in a call for Greg Handler?"

"Randy Roberts."

"Did he know him? Was he a friend?"

"Apparently, someone on the crew suggested Handler. Anders doesn't know who and he made it very clear he doesn't get involved in all the hands-on, day-to-day minutia."

I made a mental note to ask Roberts. The director had specifically told us that Scott Howell's company had sent over the cameraman. Maybe I misunderstood the conversation.

"Did he say anything at all about Ashley Amber? She said she spent that night with Londell."

And now we were hearing he spent the night playing poker.

"I asked him about Ashley and her sister. He said even though the show is struggling, Ashley's acting was helping with ratings." Em rolled her eyes as she does, not believing for a minute that the ratings had anything to do with the lady's acting skills. "But he said since Juliana Londell was out of the picture with Jason, since they'd split up, he hadn't really seen or heard much of her. I think he blamed the breakup of Jason and Juliana on Juliana. I just didn't get the feeling he had that much to share about the girl. And he was uncomfortable talking about her. My take, anyway."

"Nothing about Ashley Amber spending the night with Londell?"

"Londell and Anders talked into the night. That's all he shared."

The three of us studied our drinks at the small, round table, listening to the din of conversation around us. I even heard two people at the bar talking about the "suicide jump." We considered Anders's involvement.

Sipping my gin and tonic, I spoke to Em's interview with Anders.

Every time we get involved in a case, I look at everyone as a suspect. I just get into that mode. No matter what I think about this person or that person, they could be guilty. "So you say

Anders gets in the day before Londell leaps off the scaffolding, and immediately I'm thinking was he here to facilitate the murder? Did he want to make sure of the outcome?"

"Amigo," James said, "they were best of friends. You're my best friend, right? Would I kill you? And if I was responsible for your death, would I come down a day early just to watch you die? I don't think so."

"Skip, really," Em was pleading her case, "this guy gets a pass. He's feeling very sorry and guilty about Londell's death. He realizes that if he hadn't asked him to do a guest shot, well, you know—"

"Are you sure he gets the pass from you because he feels bad? It's not because he's handsome and charming as well? Was there possibly a little flirting going on?"

She just glared at me, not responding.

"What if you were involved with Em, James?"

"What?" He acted like I'd just accused him of murder or grand theft auto. "That's pretty far-fetched, partner."

Em smirked. "You know, I could teach you some things, James. You might be surprised."

My partner swung his attention to me.

"Pard, Clint Anders is the executive producer of *DM*. One of his best friends flew in to guest star and do him a favor."

"Yeah. Anders has a legitimate reason for being here." I was raising my voice to fight the crowd noise, but also to emphasize my point. "And so does everyone else, am I right? Let me make my point. If you want to show he was murdered, you've got to have suspects, and there doesn't seem to be a ton of them waiting in the wings. Consider this. What if Anders was interested in Ashley?"

"You're pushing it, pal."

"And he finds that Ashley is making a play for his good friend

Jason Londell. So he sees an easy way to take care of Londell and get Ashley Amber on the rebound."

"You're grasping at straws. This was a good friend."

"Yeah? Well, I saw Anders and Amber this evening, and they looked pretty cozy. His arm around her, hushed conversation—"

Em reached out and touched my hand.

"It's been a tough time for the two of them."

"You're right. But like I said, there doesn't seem to be a lot of potential killers out there."

"Except a cinematographer who took off with evidence in his camera." James frowned.

"And a young lady who probably lives twenty-three hundred miles away as the crow flies."

"Boys," Em sipped the last of her white wine and standing up, she said, "we've got our work cut out for us. If Jason Londell was killed, we need to find out how, why, and by whom. I'm with Skip. Everyone is considered a suspect until they aren't."

"Chad Rich, the grip?" James was establishing parameters.

"Everyone, James. That guy especially. He was up there."

"His partner. Jeez, we don't even know who the other grip was, do we, James?" I gave him a frown. "We don't know jack. We at least should know the two grips. It hit me earlier that you never talked to the other one."

"I'll track down Chad," James said. "He'll give me the name, and we'll do an interview. It was a slipup."

It's hard to remember James ever admitting he could slip up until now.

"In the meantime, to answer our client's main concern—"

"Where is Juliana Londell?" Em asked. "Ashley Amber wants to know if her sister killed Jason Londell. She wants to know if Juliana was sending threatening e-mails to Jason. We have yet to address her questions regarding Juliana. And we're already spending the check. Can we start thinking smart?" Em was obviously upset that we hadn't been doing enough.

"What if we call her agency?" I asked.

"Probably the first place we should have started. Boys, sometimes I wonder why we're even in this business."

I think we were all on the same page.

CHAPTER FIFTEEN

Two in the morning doesn't seem that late when you're working. Somebody still had to discourage any drunks walking home from entering our precious set and disrupting the phony surroundings we'd concocted. The flow of people was surprising to me, since I thought you went to dinner, scored, then took the girl home. All before two a.m. But, it was all only make-believe. Emily had said it best.

A stream of cars and pickups passed by at three thirty when a few bars closed, and I was confronted by a gang of five guys who pulled up in an ancient Volkswagen bus. When they rolled the window down, I could smell the pot.

"Dude, somebody took over our park."

"A TV show is all."

"Dude, we usually go out there and get a little mellow, you know?"

"Dude," I said. "find another place to get mellow. Either that or I call the cops and you will get busted for public intoxication and possession of a controlled substance. Got it?"

They moved on.

Two girls with a little too much makeup and skirts just a little too short tottered by on the sidewalk, balancing on five- or six-inch heels. "Any movie stars still up?" the short brunette asked. The closer she got, the stronger the smell from her cheap perfume.

"No movie stars tonight," I said.

"How much you got, honey?" The blonde moved closer and put her hands on my shoulders. She had to be three or four inches taller that I was, and when she looked down at me and smiled, I could count the stained, crooked teeth.

"I'm sure I don't have enough, ma'am."

"Ma'am? I'm not your momma, boy. Do you want a little action or not?"

I shook my head, suddenly aware I hadn't worked this shift before. It was a completely different group than I dealt with during the day.

"Too bad. We've had some fun with some of the others on this set."

"Been a party week," the smaller brunette burped and did a little bump and grind. "Party."

"What kind of party?" I asked.

"That trailer over there." She motioned to one of the leads' trailers. "Why, two nights ago this guy who directs things, he—"

"Directs the show?"

She ran her hands down my chest, and when she started to go further I stepped back. Her forwardness and the boozy breath mixed with sweet perfume was almost nauseating.

"Randy Roberts?"

The short girl with the black skirt looked up at her very tall friend.

"Was it a guy named Randy?"

"Oh, hell," the blonde started laughing. "There was Randy and Richard and a couple of other guys I can't remember, but I do know that Jason Londell was there in all his splendor."

"Splendor?" I shuddered.

"Look, geek boy, do you want to party or not?"

I did not. But I wanted information on previous parties.

"You ladies partied with Jason Londell?"

"Partied?" The tall blonde let go a belly laugh. "Hell, we did more than just party. We gave him a real joyride."

The smaller brunette smiled and nodded. "He was magnificent. Kept saying his wife had left him, and we were the best thing that had happened to him since then."

"Stacy was doing a reverse cowgirl, and he was shouting out his wife's name. Juliana, Juliana, then he—"

I didn't want to hear any more.

"Wait. Jason Londell said his wife left *him*?"

"He said it over and over."

"Over and over and over and, then, over," the brown-haired girl reiterated.

I had this mental image that wasn't pleasant.

"'The bitch left me. The bitch doesn't understand what she just did. The bitch left me. Juliana left *me*.' And then, the next day, he kills himself. Our little intervention didn't solve his problems. Apparently."

We'd heard that Londell left Juliana. Not the other way around. Maybe it didn't matter who did what to whom, but then again, maybe it did matter.

"Do you know who Ashley Amber is?"

"Are you kidding? We watch *Deadline Miami* religiously. And Stacy has seen every one of Ashley's movies, haven't you, girl?"

The short girl nodded. "Killer body on that bitch."

It was an awkward question, but I asked it anyway.

"Was she anywhere around when all this went down? Did she participate?"

"Oh, gawd," the blonde shrieked. "Would that have been the bomb?"

The answer was apparently "no." Ashley wasn't with the party, at least during *that* part of the evening.

"Londell told you his wife left him?"

"A guy will tell you anything to get you in the sack."

I didn't appreciate the comment.

"But once you are in the sack, most guys will level with you." The blonde with the crooked teeth leered at me.

"Why do you think that is?" I asked.

"They are so thankful that they are getting laid, they will tell you whatever you want to know. They will tell you the truth. How much they are worth. How they really feel about their wife. Once they are in the saddle, you can ask them anything and whatever they answer is pretty much the truth."

Spoken by a woman who had been there and done that.

"This Randy? He was at the party?"

"He was and he wasn't," Blondie said.

"Can you explain?"

"He was there. Big shot. 'I'm directing the show' kind of guy. But when it came to being there, he wasn't. Stacey can vouch for that."

The brunette gave me a sheepish smile.

"He didn't participate," she said.

And I realized I was second, third, or fourth string in the hierarchy. I didn't participate because I had no idea this kind of thing was going on. Randy Roberts didn't participate because he couldn't.

"Randy Roberts. Director?" I just wanted to be sure I had it right.

"Yeah, kept talking about our makeup. Too much rouge, eyeliner. Told him to take a flying fuck. Beatch. Man apparently used to be a makeup artist, before he became a big-time director, and he thinks he knows everything about a working girl's face."

"Makeup artist? That's what he told you?"

"He did."

Director, former babysitter for an actress, and a makeup artist? The guy took work wherever he could find it.

"Who else was at that party?"

"Oh, jeez," the blonde's eyes glazed over. "Just five or six guys who'd had too much to drink. We were all pretty tipsy when it was over."

"How about the young guy, blond, short hair. He was cute. You remember, the one with the black leather bracelet on his wrist? Kept asking me what made me tick," Stacy the short girl smiled.

"That's when you first showed him your boobs."

"Who was this guy?" The black leather bracelet. So maybe the camera guy on the walkway was partying with the cast, crew, and hookers. I imagined things like that going on but to actually talk to two guests of honor—

"Some guy. I think he worked the camera."

"Jerry? Jerry Clemens?" Clemens wasn't that young and he didn't have blond hair. And he didn't wear a leather bracelet. Now I was sure it was the imposter. Our fake camera guy.

"No. Don't remember his name. We were a little distracted, you know?" Reaching out, she touched my face, and I immediately wanted soap and a washcloth.

"Well, you ladies need to move on. We're not supposed to let anyone on the set tonight. Sorry."

The blonde pouted, in the dim light her painted lips showing signs of cracking. Too much lipstick, too much powder.

"Honey, you'll never know what you're missing."

"Maybe some other time."

The two ladies of the evening turned and walked back toward Em's building, and I breathed a sigh of relief. I'd never before been approached by a hooker and hoped it never happened again.

As I watched them retreat, the smaller girl turned.

"Greg. The camera guy with the black leather bracelet was Greg."

"Greg Handler?" Had to be.

"Could have been. Carry and I nicknamed him Tiny."

Her laugh lingered as the two of them walked down the sidewalk.

CHAPTER SIXTEEN

Six o'clock a.m. took forever, but when it arrived, I went up to Em's place. She answered the door in her robe, a vision of sleepiness and mussed-up hair looking very alluring. I told her about the hookers, then escorted her back to her bedroom where she made things all right again.

Finally, head propped up on two fluffed-up pillows, she looked at me and smiled.

"So, Jason Londell got it on with a prostitute his last night on earth."

"And I was under the impression that Ashley Amber was his true love. She told us that she was the one he spent the last night with."

"Maybe he made it with her later."

"Yeah, after he spent the night playing poker with Anders and Randy Roberts."

I nodded. "I should have been a movie star. Apparently, they get all the action."

"All the action? You'd give up *this*?" She pointed to herself.

"No. Jason Londell never got *this*." I gave her a fake smile. "Did he?"

"No," she teased, "but to be fair, he never asked."

"Oh, so he *could* have..."

"Londell was supposed to have been with Ashley, right?"

I nodded.

"Londell was supposedly partying with the cast last night and getting it on with a hooker, right?"

I nodded again.

"And Anders told me they'd spent part of the evening reminiscing about the old days when in fact the rumor is they were all playing poker."

"Em, technically night could go from six p.m. to six a.m. That's a lot of hours to fill. I suppose he could have been three or four places."

She smiled. "With all that activity and no rest, maybe he fell asleep up on that scaffolding." She studied me for a second. "You had Ashley in your trailer when she asked you to take the case, right?"

"Showed up on the doorstep and she was very upset."

"Skip, did Ashley really think that Londell was going to marry her?"

"I was pretty sure that she was sincere when she hired us."

"We need to know. And we need to establish a motive for his murder. We're not even close to an answer at this point."

My cell phone went off, and I checked the number. James.

"Skip, you clock out?"

"Yeah. I'm with Em. You?"

"Getting ready to report for duty. I got a little information you might be interested in, pard."

"Em and I were just saying that we don't have much information at all. Anything at this point would be welcome."

"We talked insurance, remember?"

We had.

"Anyway, there was a huge policy on Londell taken out by Anders's production company."

"James, we knew that. Roberts told me just before Londell jumped. He said that Anders was pissed about paying for the extra insurance."

"CA Productions were paying in the neighborhood of forty-eight thousand dollars a day on his coverage. Do you believe that? Forty-eight thousand dollars a day."

"But it worked out, James. The production company is being compensated. By several million dollars."

"Do you know how much several is?"

I didn't.

"Six million if it disrupts the show. Apparently, they've got to shoot some new footage since there is stuff he didn't finish. Either use a look-alike or change the plot to work around his death."

So, the show had been disrupted, and Anders's production company was getting paid six million bucks.

"Come on, James. They didn't actually expect Jason Londell to get killed. There may have been a nice payoff, but I've got to believe that Anders wishes his friend was still alive."

"Next item," James continued. "Juliana Londell had to sign a prenup."

"That's a bad thing?"

"She's still married to Londell and inherits whatever he had. Except for one condition."

"What's that?"

"That she was faithful to him."

So Londell could hang out with hard-core hookers, but the wife back home had to toe the line.

"Was she?"

"Ashley says that's the angle we should look into. She thinks Juliana might have fooled around on Londell."

It was a starting point.

"You won't believe me when I tell you how much this guy had, Skip."

"Tell me."

"Guy was mid-thirties, right? Ten years older than we are?"

"How much was his estate worth, James?"

"Around seventy-five million, give or take a few hundred thousand. Do you believe that?"

I let out a breath. Should have been a movie star. How does someone accumulate that kind of money?

"You're sure about that? That's a lot of change."

"So, let's say there's a chance she did fool around, and that fortune is in jeopardy." James was speculating.

"I know your question," I said. "Did she cover the odds with an insurance policy of her own?"

"I think one of us flies out there and checks it out. To see if Juliana was making plans for life after Jason Londell."

"He'd still have to approve it, wouldn't he? Londell would have to sign off on the bottom line. You can't just take out a huge policy on someone without them knowing about it. That would almost be a license to kill."

"Let's say I take out a policy on you, Skip, for—"

"Yeah, James, you could afford about a thirty-six dollar policy."

"Well, we need to know."

"Ashley is still up for all expenses?"

"She is."

"You talked to her recently?"

"A minute ago, pard."

"She's there? Now?"

He took a deep breath, then in a much softer voice he said, "She spent the night, amigo."

"What?"

"I wasn't going to say anything, but—"

"What?"

"Skip, settle down."

"You are a piece of work, James. Honest to God, a frigging piece of work."

"Frustrated, lonely, we had a couple of drinks and next thing you know—"

"Man, screwing the client can't be a good thing."

Em reached over and punched my arm. Hard.

"You're kidding," she whispered in a very gruff tone.

"I got some info, Skip. It gives us some direction."

"I don't believe it."

"Believe it, pally. She's very distraught about Londell's death. She just needed to be close to someone."

"All right, I'll book a flight. Em's coming too."

This time she kicked me.

"I'll see what else I can get from our client."

"Oh, I'll bet you will."

"Skip, remember, grief is nature's most powerful aphrodisiac."

I knew the quote well. Will Ferrell used it in *Wedding Crashers*.

CHAPTER SEVENTEEN

I was reminded of a great Julia Roberts movie and a quote that contained the title. "Are you sleeping with the enemy?"

It had been suggested that James do a background check on Ashley Amber. I knew very well he hadn't.

.On the surface she seemed genuine and, to be fair, she was picking up our tab, but I never counted anyone out. Em wanted to give Clint Anders a pass because he seemed *so* nice and felt so bad about his friend's death. James had slept with Ashley, so apparently he thought she passed muster. And *me*? I just wanted to solve the case. If there was a murder, then we needed a murderer, and I still believe everyone is suspect until they're not.

I did the simplest of searches, entering Google and punching in the name Ashley Amber. I found a lady in Boston who hosted a movie-review program on access cable and what looked like a porn actress named Amber Ashley, who posed in racy underwear, but there appeared to be only one Ashley Amber, actress.

She was older than I would have guessed. Thirty-two if Wikipedia was accurate. I thought she was still in her twenties. And she'd been in thirteen films and four television series. A list of commercials she'd appeared in was also listed. Deodorant, hair coloring, teeth whitening, and a push-up bra ad. I remembered that one. She'd had two words in the entire spot. "Empowering. Uplifting." I couldn't disagree. Plus, there had been some impressive video of her as well. Black lace, red lace, and pure, virginal white. And James was sleeping with her.

The interesting part was in the bio. She'd been married to an actor named Robert Courtney, some British guy whom I had never seen or heard of. She'd been seventeen, he was forty-three. Two years later he'd died, and she inherited his estate. Cause of death was not mentioned, but put forty-three into seventeen and it might be she wore him out.

Ashley's second marriage took place when she was twenty-three, and three years into that relationship the man, who had been her financial advisor, was shot in a home invasion. His wife was away on location in Idaho. Idaho? Who knew they made movies in Idaho?

Again there was no indication of how much he was worth, but the article made mention of the fact that AA was his beneficiary.

This time she wasn't married. She wasn't even officially engaged. But the first thing she ever said to me was that she and Jason Londell were close to committing to each other. And apparently committing to this actress was literally the kiss of death. I knew James had no clue, and even if he did, he'd now been bitten and would tell me the deaths were strictly coincidences. Maybe. But I worried about James. When this lady became involved with you, your chance for survival diminished greatly.

I'd proved nothing. There was a good chance these were coincidences. But the black widow spider has a reputation of mating, then killing the mate. And I'd read stories about women who were serial killers. Going from husband to husband and finding ways to hasten their demise. I just hoped Ashley wasn't one of those ladies.

CHAPTER EIGHTEEN

I'd like to say that the trip to Los Angeles was uneventful. I'd like to say that, but the truth is it was a physical and emotional roller coaster. Please understand that I'd never flown before. My heart was in my stomach, my stomach was in my bowels. At least for the takeoff. Second, Em decided, bless this sexy lady, that if expenses were in play, we should fly first class. I don't know how the other class flew, but after three Bloody Marys and a beer, I was having a great time. Possibly due to my alcoholic intake, I slept a good deal of the trip and when I did wake up, I was introduced to the Grand Canyon. I was also introduced to some severe turbulence, jolts and bumps that had the flight crew turning green. From thousands of feet in the air. OMG!

Finally, even with first-class accommodations, feeling stiff, sore, and a little out of sorts, I listened to the pilot saying—

"Ladies and gentlemen, to the right, you'll see Thousand Oaks, California."

He kept his travelogue going over a thirty-minute period. He was obviously familiar with the topography and very proud of his knowledge of this geographic area.

"The famous community of Malibu."

And again with, "Pacific Coast Highway, that ribbon you see winding around the ocean."

And Santa Monica, downtown L.A., and even the Los Angeles River. Who knew L.A. had its own river? I didn't. Em knew it, because she's traveled a whole lot more than I have.

"Ladies and gentlemen, if you look out your right-hand window, we are approaching LAX, on runway twenty-four R."

It meant nothing to me or to anyone else in the plane, but this pilot liked to hear himself talk. "We are now cruising at ten million feet and will level off at four zillion yards and—" Who cares?

When I heard the motorized whining sound and felt a thump, I froze, grasping the armrest. Em assured me it was the landing gear being lowered, and the only time to panic was when you didn't hear it.

The plane came down hard, and it was only after about fifteen seconds that I opened my eyes. Em was laughing.

We got off, all carry-on luggage due to the insight of my amazing girlfriend, and walked to the transportation area. No bags, no baggage fees. It was almost too smooth, and I secretly said a prayer, thanking some Supreme Being for having Emily there to walk me through the problem areas.

Thirty minutes later, we were at the Hollywood Express, a not-too-ostentatious accommodation, but Em told me it beat the hell out of a Motel Six. I simply nodded, having no basis for argument.

Unpacking the few clothes and toiletries I'd brought, I pulled open the heavy drapes and stared out at the pitted parking lot, a lonesome palm tree and the brown Chevy Aveo we'd rented. A step up from my set of wheels and a big step down from Emily's vehicle.

"Boyfriend, we need to have an agenda."

I couldn't argue.

"Number one, find Juliana Londell."

"Got it."

"Number two, find out if she took out a large life insurance policy on her husband."

"Got it."

"Number three, get the financial report on those two and a copy of the prenup. Not that I give that much hope but—"

My phone buzzed.

"James, we've arrived."

"Seen any movie stars?"

"They're all in Miami this week, James."

"Skip, coroner's report is out."

"Finally. You've seen it?"

"No. We'll get a copy, but I do know what the foreign substance in Jason Londell's body was."

"You want to share?" I put him on speakerphone. I was certain it was some sort of hallucinogen.

"Sure. The foreign substance was lead."

"Lead?" What? Did he suck on his painted crib rail as a child? Lead poisoning wasn't that common and—

"Like a twenty-two slug. It went in under his chin and lodged in his brain. The body was so torn up from the fall they didn't catch the wound at first. Somebody shot him, Skip. Up close and personal."

"My God, it really was murder."

"Told ya."

"Next item on the agenda," Em said, "is to find cameraman Greg Handler. And, James, you'd better find that other grip. That's on you."

CHAPTER NINETEEN

She had an office. I was under the impression she worked out of her home, but it turns out Juliana had an office, a secretary, and another agent with a desk and everything. James and I worked off of a very small dining room table in our crappy apartment and took calls on my cell phone.

This office was in a professional building about ten minutes from our motel. It took forty-five minutes to get there. I'd always heard L.A. traffic was a mess most of the time.

The subtle sign on the building boasted an accounting firm, a travel agency, a music company, and a company called Flippin' Films. Inside, the engraved sign on their door simply stated Londell/Bavely Talent Representation.

I glanced at Em and shrugged my shoulders. We probably should have planned ahead, but in this case we had no idea what to expect. I opened the door and we walked in.

The lady at the front desk was startled.

"We rarely have walk-ins," she said. "Our secretary is out temporarily, but what can I help you with?"

I glanced around. There were two hard-back chairs and several copies of *Variety* and *Billboard* on a small table in the corner. Framed copies of *Rolling Stone* magazine covers, *People* magazine covers and photos of famous and semifamous actors decorated the walls, and I noticed conspicuous vacant spaces between the pieces. I immediately decided those were spots where Jason Londell or other ex-clients had been prominently featured.

Had been.

"We're looking for Juliana Londell." Em said.

"She's not here. Can I tell her what this is regarding?"

Glancing at Em, I saw her brow crease, signaling thinking stage.

"I would like to talk about representation."

The girl's eyes widened.

My eyes widened.

She appraised Em, almost deliberately, starting at her tanned legs, then up to the short skirt and her thin waist. I watched her eyes wander up past the chest to the sculpted face and mass of blonde highlighted hair. She smiled.

"Juliana isn't accepting any new clients at this moment."

Em nodded, a coy smile on her face.

"I believe I could convince her."

"If you'd like to leave a head shot and résumé?"

Em glanced at me. I knew immediately I'd have to find a quick print place and take some fast photos.

"If she's not accepting any new clients, why would I leave any information about myself?"

"You are very attractive," the woman said. "If you would please leave your information—"

"You just said she's not accepting any new clients." Em was affecting an attitude, which wasn't exactly strange to her.

"She's not," the woman said in a condescending tone.

"Then?"

"But *I* am. I'm Kathy Bavely, and I would be interested in

talking to you. Do you have head shots and a bio?" She thrust a business card into Em's hand.

"No," I blurted out, "not with us, but we'll be back with whatever information you need."

I turned and Em followed. We walked out as the lady shouted after us.

"I hope you'll come back. I like what I see."

CHAPTER TWENTY

"We could have just said we were P.I.s and asked for an appointment. Wouldn't that have been a lot simpler?"

"True, and she could have said no. What did you want to do, Skip? Tip her off that we were investigating her?"

"I'm sure the cops are investigating her. Isn't the spouse always the first suspect in a murder case?"

She ignored me.

"Look, you still didn't get an appointment with Juliana, Em. Now we've got to pretend that we're—"

"I was trying to get some leverage, Skip."

"By what? Pretending to be an actress? Where is that going to lead us? What good is that going to do?"

"I don't know, but with you as my manager, we'll see, won't we? If we don't solve the case, at least I may make a decent living as a movie star." She flipped her soft blonde hair back and gave me a bright smile.

"Really?"

"I won't pretend I haven't thought about it."

"Since when?" I'd known her since high school and never heard Em talk about going "Hollywood." "You've never said anything about acting. Other than the lead in *Bye Bye Birdie* in high school—"

"Every girl fantasizes about being a princess. In this country, the closest you get to princess is movie star." She paused, "Well, Grace Kelly found a way to be both, but come on, Skip, you've never dreamed of being—James Bond or Jason Bourne?"

I'd dreamed of being every superhero in comic book kingdom. Imagined I was every spy in the world and every movie action hero in the last fifteen years, but only dreamed. And here, with one phony call, Em was close to actually getting an agent and fulfilling her fantasy.

Fat chance of that ever happening. No résumé, no head shots.

Here we were in the land of make-believe, pretending to be private investigators, pretending to solve a violent murder in Miami while pretending to be actress and her manager. We fit in very well.

The strip mall store advertised passport photos and head shots in their window. Five digital photos, ten copies, and we were out the door for fifty bucks. I could have done the same on my cell phone, but this guy seemed to know what agents wanted.

"This is the style and these are the poses they look for," he said. "And, lady, you are the real deal." His eyes explored her body. "They're looking for you." He leered at Em, wetting his lips. "And, hey, if you ever want to do something a little racier, here's my card."

We left, photos in my right hand, middle finger extended on my left hand.

A believable résumé was another thing.

Inside a FedEx office location, Em worked the Internet.

"Here's a sample," she pointed to the screen. "Sort of a template. TV roles, movies, theater, commercials, training, and special skills."

"Why don't we start with the special skills," I said. "There's that thing you do in the shower when—"

"Seriously?"

"Okay, what kind of roles have you had?"

"How about policewoman in *Deadline Miami*, recurring role?"

"Wow. I like that. You're one of the background officers."

"What else, Skip? You watch TV. There must be other obscure roles I could have had."

"James watches Ellen DeGeneres. Put down that you have played various characters in skits. You were a dancer, or you took one of the audience members on a crazy trip through Wal-Mart. Ellen does some bizarre stuff."

"Okay, have I done theater?"

"Sure. You were Off Broadway in—" and I realized I didn't know much about theater. "You haven't done theater, except for playing the Ann-Margret role of Kim MacAfee in *Bye Bye Birdie* in high school—God she had been sexy in that role—but you were a shopkeeper in *Entourage*, a waitress in *According to Jim*," and so it went as we put together Em's professional life. I had no idea if this agent would check on her, but the roles were sketchy, almost all just walk-ons, so I figured Kathy Bavely wouldn't look into Em's background too hard.

Em had been girl number three in a Chili's ad, a surprised socialite in an Ashton Kutcher Nikon camera commercial, and she'd even had a conversation with Chad in the Verizon television spots. Everyone important seemed to have hired her to represent their company, but she was almost always background. Barely recognizable.

Theater training was at a small community college in Miami, and I listed her as taking private lessons with a famous director who had died last year. They couldn't check on that.

"Special skills," Em paused, "and not the one you're thinking of," she said.

"Acting skills? You took ballet as a kid."

"I dance pretty well. We'll put it down. Anything else?"

"Nothing I can think of. Other than—"

"How about firearms," she said.

"Firearms?" I had no idea what she was talking about.

"Yeah. I took a conceal and carry class two months ago. It turns out I'm a pretty good shot."

I was stunned.

"And when were you going to tell me this?" Was she making this up or did she really take the course?

"I don't know. It was eight hours and just one of those private things. I didn't want to make a big deal out of it."

She surprised me. All the time. And here James and I were licensed private investigators and had no permits to carry weapons. I'd definitely have to look into a concealed permit.

When we finally had the background, Em formatted it until it looked like the sample template on the Internet, and we printed up five copies. I was impressed.

"You're bona fide."

"I was *bona fide* the last time we were together at my place."

Now she was the one getting risqué.

I ignored her lewd comment. "So, now what?"

"We go to Kathy Bavely tomorrow and give her the head shots and résumé. Let's see if I can get representation."

"Em, where is this going?"

"Skip, I'm winging this. You of all people should understand." She shook her head as if to insinuate I was an idiot for not understanding. "We need to get to know Juliana Londell and find out whether she stands to collect on an insurance policy."

"We could have asked."

"If she's involved, she's not going to notify us. At this point, the way we've positioned ourselves with me possibly being Kathy's client, we're in Juliana's space. If I become, even for an instant, an important person in this space, we stand a chance to find information. We're going to be in the same office, and I feel certain we're going to meet the woman. I'm just going to go with the flow."

"Isn't that a phrase from the sixties? Go with the flow?"

"Skip, I'm a rising star in the present. I'm going to light up the world. You name the number one twenty-something pop star, and I'm going to be light years ahead of them. Got it?"

She smiled at me, a look that was very sincere.

"We're going to find out if Ashley Amber's sister is responsible for Jason Londell's murder."

I nodded, hoping this was the end result.

"And," she added, "we're going to find out if I have what it takes to be an American princess."

I think she was halfway serious.

CHAPTER TWENTY-ONE

Our final stop came from a website I'd visited regarding a SAG-AFTRA card. As I understood it, after an actor had a speaking role in a union production whether it's a movie, TV role, or commercial, he has thirty days to get a union card, or he couldn't get a role in another union production. It was part of the Taft-Hartley Act, and I had no idea what that was.

Since we'd dummied up a résumé, Em had to show some proof that she was a member of SAG-AFTRA. We weren't actually interested in a role, because by the time agent Kathy Bavely started pitching Emily to producers, we'd be back in Miami, hopefully with enough information to decide if Juliana Londell had taken an active role in killing her husband.

The place was a print shop in a very sketchy part of town, and they advertised SAG cards as a novelty gift. "Impress your friends," the ad said. "Show them you are a certified actor with this look-alike card."

"How look-alike is this card?" I asked.

The young guy with a sparse beard, his pants too low, and a sideways baseball cap smirked.

"You won't be able to tell the difference, dude."

I'd never seen a SAG card so he was dead-on about that.

When he was finished, I hoped that Kathy the agent would buy it. Better yet, I hoped she would never ask. With a good résumé, I hoped she'd just assume that we had the card. After all, how did Em get all these juicy roles?

"If we get outed, we just go a different direction," Em said.

I had to admire her determination. She was really getting into the part.

Half an hour later, the young guy brought out the card. Blue and tan, with a logo on the left that showed a line drawing of a smiling face and a frowning face. I guess that was acting. Happy or sad. No middle ground.

Very official looking.

Screen Actors Guild. Associated Actors and Artists of America/ AFL-CIO.

And there was her name, Emily Minard, her very own identification number, and a statement that she'd joined two years ago. The cocky kid had even laminated the card to keep it shiny and new.

We were back on the sidewalk, walking toward our rental, and in the small grassy plot to my left, I saw McDonald's wrappers and discarded Styrofoam cups, dozens of plastic bags, and empty cigarette packs. Empty beer bottles littered the area and ahead the sidewalk was pitted, cracked, and stained with brown splotches and patches that appeared to be blood red. A mangy, gray-haired dog, thin as a stick, prowled the lot with a low growl in his throat, watching every step we took. Not the glitz and glamour Hollywood experience I'd expected.

"Hey, boyfriend. I'm an actress. And it only cost about sixty bucks. All right, Mr. DeMille, I'm ready for my close-up."

I recognized the quote from *Sunset Boulevard* with Gloria Swanson. An oldie but a goodie. It had been made into a

Broadway play, and I should have made her a character in that play on her résumé. Oh, well, if we ever updated that sheet of paper.

We were both pleased.

We had dinner at Dan Tana's on Santa Monica Boulevard. Long known for its celebrity clientele and great food, it seemed like a place to go when you're on an expense account. Dark wood, red padded booths, and red-and-white checkered tablecloths, the glamour days of Hollywood were still alive.

At the bar we had a Cosmopolitan and a beer before dinner when we realized a guy who used to be on TV long before we were born was four seats down from us. I never would have known who he was, but a patron pointed him out to us.

"Guy played Linc on *The Mod Squad*. Remember? Clarence Williams the Third?"

Linc? We had no clue.

I did recognize the actor who played The Rock. Dwayne Johnson, he of the sculptured physique. He was sequestered in a far corner of the restaurant engaged in intimate conversation with a beautiful Asian woman. We were sandwiched between a Linc and a Rock. Don't ask me to explain.

Christian, the maître d', ushered us to a spot by the kitchen, where important people weren't seated. The doors flew open every ten or fifteen seconds, and the raw odors of dozens of dishes wafted to our table, some good and some not so good.

"Well, at least this dining experience is all paid for," Em said.

"They don't know you're a superstar. If they saw that résumé, those head shots, we'd have the best table in the house."

"Tomorrow everyone will know," she said. "Girl number three in a Chili's ad. Whatever. I'm surprised they're not lined up at our table for autographs."

Em ordered chicken cacciatore, and I had a New York strip

steak. At prices I never would have paid, even if it had been my money. Thank God, it wasn't. James was going to be very jealous. He was a culinary major and dreamed of visiting iconic restaurants in the United States to see if they matched their reputations. This one, in my humble opinion, did. The food, the service, they were impeccable. However, at these prices they should be.

"All right, Em. We walk in tomorrow. This Bavely chick agrees to rep you. Then what?"

"Here's what I've been thinking."

I was glad one of us was thinking. At this time I had no idea what we were going to do.

She sipped her second Cosmo, tilting her head back to let the triple sec-lime juice-cranberry vodka mix slide down her throat.

"Juliana has a professional office, so chances are she keeps files. On her computer, certainly, but paper files as well. Skip, you and I already have paper files on my acting career and we just started. Already we have a paper résumé, photographs, and this union card. If we have files, trust me, she'll have files."

I nodded, still not certain where this was going.

"She owns this business. It's her agency, so I think she keeps personal files as well as business files. If you're organizing one side of your life, why not organize the other side of your life in the same space?"

"You think it's that simple? She's got her insurance policy in her office in a paper file? It's right under our nose?"

"My dad does," she said very matter-of-fact. "In his office, he keeps his personal papers in a file drawer where he keeps business deals, information on vendors, collection reports—he owns his business and it's more convenient for him to have all his personal stuff right there too."

"So you're suggesting—"

"Somehow, I'll distract. You go through the files. You distract, I'll do the same. Let's try to get Bavely and Londell out of the immediate area, and we'll check out files, desk information, anything we can learn."

"I can't believe there isn't an easier way to find out."

"Think of one. I have no idea what insurance company she would use. Where do you begin to look for something like that? And the other thing is, Ashley asked us to check on the unfaithful angle, remember? If we had access to her files or her computer or cell phone, I would think we stand a good chance of seeing if there was or is a relationship going on with someone else."

Em was right. If, and if was a big part of this, if we could explore her social life, we could see if she had another love life.

"It's not like we haven't broken laws before."

"I know, I know," she said. "There's always a slim chance we could get caught. I mean, there are no perfect plans."

"And then what?"

"With my charm? Come on, Skip. All I have to do is blink my eyes, pout my lips and—" Her eyes left mine and drifted over my shoulder. I glanced back and the muscular actor Dwayne Johnson was walking by. His attractive Asian companion had stopped to talk to two men at a table near ours, and Johnson stopped at Emily's chair.

"You are a very beautiful woman." He placed a hand on her shoulder. "Striking. You should be in pictures."

I was sitting right there, totally ignored.

She beamed her headlight smile at him.

"If you only knew," she said.

CHAPTER TWENTY-TWO

Making love in a city almost three thousand miles from home didn't make it any different. Distance didn't seem to make the experience more intense, but making love to a bona fide actress, that was off the charts. This lady had been an extra in an Ashton Kutcher Nikon Camera commercial and here I was naked with her in bed. Hot stuff.

Making love to someone that Dwayne Johnson found very attractive? A very heady experience. I was in rare company and totally aware of that. Emily was a special person on many levels, and why she chose to spend her charms with me, I have no idea. It's always been a mystery.

After a steamy encounter, one that seemed to relive some of our passion from the last forty-eight hours, we both took a breather, staring at a dark, flat screen mounted in the armoire.

"That was pretty intense," she said. Thank God, she spoke first.

"We're both in a fragile state. Not sure what we are doing and not quite sure if this new idea will work." I put my arm around her nude body, caressing her soft, tanned skin.

"Dwayne Johnson thought I was hot, Skip. The Rock."

I got up and went to the bathroom, returning in my jeans and T-shirt. Walking down to the Coke machine, I reflected on what we were doing. Em had actually devised an interesting way of getting close to Juliana Londell. What we'd planned was devious, underhanded, and illegal. Em's grand idea had James written all over it, and that scared me.

I brought back a Diet Coke and an orange soda, plus a Hershey bar. We'd both worked up somewhat of an appetite.

"Look, Skip, Jay Leno has Logan Lerman on."

She'd turned on the TV and was sitting up in bed, topless, adjusting the volume.

"He's here, in town."

"And?" I questioned her point.

"I mean, think about it. They're all here. This is the movie capital of the world. I'm saying, within ten miles of us, there are hundreds of movie stars. You and James, you trade movie quotes like girls trade clothes or jewelry. And this is where they come from. Those quotes. Pretty cool."

It was pretty cool. And tomorrow, I was going to accompany someone who'd always wanted to be an actress, to her first audition. And together, we'd see if we could pull it off. If she could convince Kathy Bavely that she was an actress. We'd find out if Emily Minard, after one day in Hollywood, could convince a talent agent to represent her. When thousands of would-be actors went agentless every day. Yes, tomorrow would be very interesting.

I thought there was a good chance she could pull it off. There were times I thought she was going through the motions even with me. And I fell for it every time.

And as for Dwayne Johnson, yes, that encounter was still on my mind. I'd seen him in *The Tooth Fairy*, and the man could not act his way out of a tutu. The only thing that muscle-bound idiot had going for him was his good taste in women.

• • •

I woke up early. Eight o'clock Miami time, five o'clock in L.A. Walking outside, I marveled at how different and yet the same Los Angeles and Miami were. The freshness of the morning air was tainted with the stale odor of exhaust and smog. Palm trees and concrete, impersonal cement-block and stucco-covered buildings sprung up everywhere and just looking down the street we were on, I could see the ugly urban sprawl. Miami, for all the current attempts at being the cultural center of the South, was still trying to find itself, with a serious case of urban sprawl and decay of its own.

But there was a swagger to L.A. that I'd already picked up on. I could feel it in the people that we'd met, the businesses that we'd visited. This was a city that was street-smart. It was a movie capital and it knew that everything was pretend, just for show, and you got a sense that the city and the people who lived here believed they could get away with just about anything.

Even a murder, clear across the continent.

They could get away with just about anything here, and I hoped that swagger and attitude rubbed off on us.

When I got back to the motel, Emily was dressed in some very stylish yellow Capri pants and a top that bared her stomach. It appeared as if she'd tied a flower-patterned scarf over her breasts and that was it. With her blonde hair swept back and just a hint of makeup, Em was ready to take on Hollywood.

I couldn't take my eyes off of her, and neither could the people we passed as we walked to a small breakfast bar down the block.

"Do I get the part?" she asked.

I took a second gulp of coffee before I answered.

"If you don't get it, I want to meet the lady who does. You are breathtaking, Em. Breathtaking."

"It's nice to hear, even if you are somewhat prejudiced."

An hour later we drove the car back to Juliana's office and walked in.

I glanced into the far office and saw Bavely at her desk. A tall, thin brunette was busy filing papers in the far room.

Glancing at Em, I whispered, "Can't be Juliana. Not if she's pregnant. Must be the missing secretary."

"Well, hello." Kathy Bavely looked right past me to Em.

"I'm back."

"Oh, I can see that."

I reached over the desk and handed her a manila envelope with copies of the head shots and two copies of her résumé.

"Sit down. Let me look at these."

Leafing through the photos, she nodded. "Not bad, but we'd have to get more expressions. And maybe do the hair in a number of styles. Still," she studied one in particular, "you don't take a bad picture, do you?"

Em just smiled.

"Well, I see you've done some work, obviously nothing to brag about, but you've got a foundation." Pursing her lips, she dismissed the résumé and studied Em for a long ten or fifteen seconds.

"You've got a SAG card?"

Reaching into her purse, Em pulled the newly minted card from her wallet.

"That's good enough. It appears you're serious about this career."

"I know the parts I've had are pretty sketchy, but I really am a very good actress. When I take on a role, it becomes mine. I live it, I breathe it, I believe it, and—" She paused.

"And?" Bavely asked.

"The audience believes *me*. I'm very believable. And isn't that what this business is all about?"

The lady nodded, starting with a slight nod then moving her head up and down with a serious appreciation for what she'd just heard. Hell, I was nodding. Em had proven to me she was an actress. I'd never seen Em pretend so convincingly. Well, once in a while I thought she was faking it, but—

"If we develop this relationship," Bavely tapped one of the photos on her desk, "you would sign a contract."

"Of course."

"You would be available for casting calls almost any time of the day and sometimes the evening. This can be a twenty-four-hour business, Miss Minard. From casting calls to acting jobs."

"Understood."

"You would take my advice, get new head shots, and treat this as a career choice, not a game."

"Yes."

"One final thing I want you to do."

"Okay."

"I want you to come back after lunch. Let's say, two o'clock."

"I can do that," Em said.

There was no 'the two of you.' I may as well not have been there.

"I have to run you by Juliana." Bavely rolled her eyes. "I told you she isn't accepting new clients, but she has to pass approval on anyone I sign. It's—" she paused taking a deep breath, "it's the way it is."

"So," I asked, "this isn't a partnership?"

She turned away from us, not answering the question.

"Just be here. Okay?"

"Should I be a little worried that she won't like me?"

Kathy Bavely studied Em again, like a butcher would size up a lamb chop, giving both of us the creeps.

"Oh, she'll like you. Trust me. I'm positive of that."

We, or at least Em, were going to meet Ashley Amber's sister,

Jason Londell's wife and the soon-to-be mother of Jason Londell's child. This introduction was going to be very interesting.

She did a little shopping. Em wanted to see what Rodeo Drive was all about and she had the money to do it. I made a quick call to James, letting him know what was happening.

"She's what?"

"Got an agent. Juliana's partner is going to rep her. I can't believe it happens like this, but it does."

"You're nuts. Crazy. What the hell are you two thinking? This is off the chart, Skip. There's got to be an easier way to get that information."

"James." He was hot, but I was calm and collected. I needed to settle him down and I knew how to do it. "This is exactly what you would have done."

"Yeah? You think?" He hesitated, the overheated passion in his voice cooling down in a matter of seconds.

"No question. You would seize the moment and jump right in. You know it, I know it. It's your trademark. When in doubt, fake it."

"Okay, you're right." Subdued in less than a minute. "Just hurry up, pardner. Things are a little tense back here."

"Tense?"

"Security isn't happy that you aren't here. You're still under contract, you know, and there's some question about where you are and what you're doing."

I did know I was under contract.

"I haven't told anyone the truth, Skip. They think it's a touch of the flu. But we're short a man, and the sooner you can get answers to your questions—"

"There's no guarantee, James. We're making this up as we go."

"The story of our lives, Tonto."

He was right. We were always floating on the edge of lunacy.

"Get busy, amigo."

"It's only been a day, my friend."

I told him about Dan Tana's and could hear him sigh.

"It's a landmark, Skip. The food had to be really good, am I right? Don't tell me it wasn't just about perfect."

"Perfect? It's the place that Dwayne Johnson hit on Em, James."

"No shit? Dwayne Johnson? The actor? He really hit on her?"

"It's the truth."

My business partner paused. "The truth? You can't handle the Tooth. And that's the whole Tooth and nothing but the Tooth."

I cringed remembering the quote. Even he remembered how bad Johnson had been in *The Tooth Fairy*.

"Skip, I was going to call you. Seriously. I'm just doing a final check on this thing and—"

"What thing?"

"Well, it might be *anything*." He paused, and I knew he didn't want to tell me the story. "Don't freak out when I explain this to you, okay?"

"What are you talking about?"

"I got a hold of Chad Rich."

"The grip."

"The same."

"And?"

"I was supposed to get info on the other grip, right? His assistant was a guy named Andy Hall."

"Don't tell me this guy was a phony. Make-believe driver's license, bad makeup job. Don't even."

"No. Rich had worked with him before."

"So, you finally got to talk to this Andy Hall?"

"I wish."

107

"You're dragging this out, partner."

"This Hall guy didn't show up for work yesterday. And Rich says he's pretty reliable, so Rich started looking into it. This guy Hall lived by himself, a loner, so there was no one he was accountable to."

"Give, James."

"Chad Rich finally drove over to the place this Andy Hall rents. Guy doesn't stay on site."

"Yeah?"

"He knocks on the door and no one answers."

James's narrative was sounding like a cheap mystery novel.

"James, give me the details. Please."

"Bottom line is, he turns the doorknob and the door opens. It's not locked and he just walks in."

"He walks in and finds what?"

"Andy Hall, front and center."

"Alive? Or dead?"

"It appears that Andy Hall had committed suicide."

Suicide. I was tired of hearing the word. Shivering, I held the receiver at arm's length and considered the possibilities.

"Rich found a bottle of pills. Looks like the guy overdosed on prescription medication."

I was quiet for a moment, thinking of the hopelessness that must be in some people's lives. To want to end it all just seems so foreign to me. Someone apparently loads up on negatives.

Me, I keep looking at the positives.

"Cops are looking into it? Tying it into Londell's murder?"

"Obviously, they don't consult me on a regular basis, but the people on set are conspiracy theorists. They figure it's suicide or someone killed him because he knew too much. He was up there, Skip. One of the few. You were down below, one of the few. He's probably not a person of interest." Pausing, James said, "Well, any more than you are, but someone fired that twenty-two-caliber bullet, and there were only four people up there. Am I right?"

He was.

"So two of the four people on that catwalk are dead and one has disappeared, am *I* right?"

"What are the odds?" James asked.

"James," thoughts were racing through my head, "the two hookers I met by the park, the ones who partied with Londell—"

"Thanks for clarifying. You meet so many hookers."

"Trying to make a point here, so kindly shut up. These two remembered Randy Roberts, telling me he was not a participant. I think they were saying the guy couldn't perform. Anyway, he ended up criticizing them for their makeup. Told them he used to be a makeup artist before he became a director and he did not approve of the way they looked."

"Andy Hall committed suicide, Skip. He was the second grip on the scaffolding. What the hell does this Randy Roberts story have to do with anything?"

"Randy Roberts did makeup. What if he was the guy who dressed up with the big nose and mustache and rented the camera? The guy who stole a company credit card and pretended to be Greg Handler?"

"Interesting take, amigo, but why does the death of Andy Hall remind you of Randy Roberts?"

"James, I'm remembering that Randy Roberts told me a story about visiting an actress in her trailer half an hour before she overdosed and killed herself. I'm starting to connect the dots."

CHAPTER TWENTY-THREE

"Do me a favor and check out an actress named Audrey Love."

"You're making up names?"

"No. That's the actress who died of an overdose. Roberts was telling me the cops tried to hang it on him. Do you remember that conversation I had on the phone with him?"

"Sort of."

"On the phone that night, he told me this story about baby-sitting some actors several years ago, and he said he'd been in this Audrey Love's trailer half an hour before someone found her dead of a drug overdose."

"Come on, man, Randy Roberts did not kill Jason Londell. You know it, I know it. He was on the ground directing the shot."

"And Londell's wife was twenty-three hundred miles away in California. Why am I here if location means you are innocent?"

"Point well taken. You're right, man. Sorry."

"Get what you can online, okay? About Randy Roberts the director, and Audrey Love, the actress. And watch your back. There's some strange shit going on, James. Believe me."

"Amigo, you are the one who witnessed the murder. You saw something that most of us did not. You actually saw someone shoot the actor. You didn't realize it, but you saw it happen. So watch *your* back."

I knew he was right. And there was something gnawing at me, something I did see and I couldn't remember. Something else that happened in that compressed moment that I knew I'd recall sooner or later. For the sake of the case, for the sake of my safety, I hoped I'd remember it sooner.

CHAPTER TWENTY-FOUR

After Em threw four fancy designer fashion bags in the backseat, we drove back to Londell and Bavely's, arriving at one thirty, and I parked half a block from the office. Em sipped her Starbucks mocha and I watched the people walking the sidewalk. We wanted to see this Juliana before she saw us. Kind of get a heads-up on what kind of a woman she was.

The two of us settled on 104.3 FM radio, a mix of current hits with some music from several years ago. Mostly, the station carried an advertising where-to-go menu for Los Angeles. Mirando Casino, *less than ninety minutes from wherever you are.* Loma Linda Medical University Center, *treating over ten thousand cancer patients per year*, Excalibur Hotel and Casino with the male revue *Thunder from Down Under*, Dick's Last Resort, and Newport Beach. Commercial after commercial after commercial.

Em rolled her eyes.

"Isn't there a station that actually plays some music now and then?"

The next spot told us to look forward to tomorrow morning

when *Valentine in the Morning* would regale us with his clever patter on the A.M. show.

"I look forward to a little bit of *Moore in the Morning*," Em said, her hand resting on my thigh.

To be fair, on the present *Kari Steele Show* there was a little music thrown in. Not much, but some.

"So, do you think this Andy Hall really killed himself?"

"I'm the guy who swore that Jason Londell committed suicide. That shows you how much I know."

"Skip, what if this Hall guy was part of the murder?"

"Or he knew who was behind it?"

"Maybe Chad Rich had a hand in it."

"No, Em, I get a pretty good feel for Rich. I know what I said about thinking everyone is a suspect, but I think he's as confused as anyone."

"So either it was an accident, someone decided to take him out, or he killed himself because he was guilty?"

"He was up there. One of three people pulled the trigger because I don't think Jason Londell shot himself."

I shrugged my shoulders. Too many ifs.

"Is that her?" I watched an attractive brunette walking toward the building led by a long, sleek dog on a leash.

"Too thin."

"She's what? James said three months? Do women show at that stage?"

She turned to me and frowned.

"How the hell would I know?"

Several more women walked by, no guys. There was a yogurt shop on the corner, a dry cleaner, Laundromat combination in the next block, and a pet store beside our car. Pedestrians continued to pass by, but no one appeared to be Juliana Londell.

"If we ever—"

"Get married?" Em read my mind.

"Yeah. Would there be any preexisting conditions? Unfaithfulness or a prenup that said you couldn't have—"

Her eyes popped open. "I couldn't have what? *You've* got nothing. Let's turn that around, okay? I couldn't have? Give me a break."

"I just meant that—"

"Just drop it." I'd hit a sore spot. "Maybe there's another way to get into that office that we're not aware of."

"Maybe there's a rear entrance and a parking lot in the back." It was an idea.

"Could be, but I think that's her." Em pointed to a green Jag XKE that pulled in front of the building. A dark-haired girl had gotten out, walked around to the driver's side, and lip-locked the driver, for at least five or six seconds.

"What makes you say that?"

"Loose serape top over jeans. Kind of hides the early baby bump."

"Ah, you who doesn't know when a woman shows."

"It's her, Skip. And she appears to be very into the good-looking guy with the green sports car."

She did.

"So," I said, having already analyzed the situation, "does that count as unfaithful? The kissing thing?"

"I'm not a legal scholar, Skip, but the husband is dead. The will, stating that she must be faithful to inherit, is probably null and void. But don't take my word for it. Maybe she has to be faithful unto her own death."

The lady walked into the building, and we waited another fifteen minutes before we ventured forth.

"Emily. Thank you for coming back." Kathy Bavely was all smiles, again ignoring the fact that I even existed.

"Have a seat and I'll make sure Juliana is ready to see you," she said.

I noticed she stretched the name Juliana a little too long, an affected negative sound on the widow's name.

"By the way, let me ask you a strange personal question. Do you have a dog?"

I saw the light go on in Em's eyes.

"I do. I love dogs."

She didn't. And she didn't.

"I had a feeling," Bavely said, a big grin on her face. "I trust people who love dogs. You know what I mean? I've got a mix. A Yorkie and silky, name of Brilliant Bentley. Don't you just love it?"

"I'm dog crazy," Em said, gushing with enthusiasm. "I named my miniature schnauzer Skip, after my manager." She pointed to me and it was the first time I felt like I'd actually mattered in this strange relationship. "He yaps a lot, but usually does exactly what I tell him." So smug.

Bavely laughed and turned to me. "You're the manager?"

"I am." *What the hell do you think I am, lady? Window dressing?*

Cocking her head, she smiled and asked, "Do you get along with Emily's dog, Mr. Manager?"

"Skip is wonderful with," Em paused, "Skip." She laughed, and I thought about my relationship with her dog. The dog that didn't exist, but due to Em's heroic acting skills I believed. I just hoped that Bavely did as well. This was coming along better than I had dreamed because, to be honest, I thought we were way out of our league here. Em was actually pulling it off. What, I wasn't sure.

"I really think this relationship is going to work," Kathy Bavely said, "assuming," she paused, frowning a little, "well, just let me get Juliana." There was almost a little fear in her voice.

A moment later, Bavely walked out with a very attractive brunette in a red, yellow, and green Mexican print serape hanging over jeans. The lady was a knockout, and I knew what a knockout was. I was dating one. Em had nailed her. It was the lady hiding the "baby bump," as Em called it. My girlfriend was always one, two, three, or four steps ahead of me.

Juliana Londell oozed good looks, but any charm and personality she might have possessed were quickly forgotten.

"You're the unknown Emily Minard?"

"I am," Em said.

"You almost have a negative history. Do you know that?" She practically glared at my girlfriend. "You've worked for some of the most notable companies and productions in the industry, and you've been relegated to totally forgettable background status." She shook her head. "What the hell were you thinking? Is that seriously the best you could do?"

Arms folded across her chest, she squinted her eyes and stared at Em, shaking her head.

"Poor management, poor representation. Very sad."

We were a success. The résumé was so weak, it wasn't even questioned. I smiled, since no one was paying any attention to me anyway.

"I can't deny that," Em said. "But that's why I need some awesome representation. That's why I came to you." Pointing at Londell, she said, "You are the reps to get me positioned for bigger roles."

"Wouldn't do you much good to deny it." Londell studied her, saying, "I can't even find much about you on the Internet."

I knew for a fact that the lady couldn't find *anything* on her. Em had a low profile and wasn't even on Facebook, Twitter, or LinkedIn. When there was success in her father's company, he was the one who got the credit. Em laid low.

"However," Londell continued, "we'd like to send you out on a couple of casting calls. It's the best way we can get a feel for how people are going to react to you. You've certainly got the looks, and you seem to carry yourself well, but whether you can act is another story."

I looked at Em, the question in my eyes. Was Juliana Londell taking over? Was Kathy Bavely simply the finder? I remembered James telling me the lady took what she wanted.

"I'm ready to prove myself," Em nodded, a faint smile on her lips.

"Well, Kathy," she nodded to her partner, "I think she's a keeper. I like the look and attitude. I'll work with you on developing this talented lady, and we'll just see how far she can go."

The office felt like a meat factory as I watched Juliana run her eyes over Em again. These two ladies seemed overly interested in my girlfriend's body.

"Why don't the three of us go into your office and—" She seemed to notice me for the first time.

"I'm sorry. You are?"

"I'm Skip Moore. I'm Em's manager."

"Mmmm. How long have you been her manager?"

"Long enough." I didn't like her tone.

"Long enough to see her career go nowhere?" She once again crossed her arms and gave me a long, hard look. "I'm sorry, but if you're working on a percentage, Mr. Moore, is it? If you're working on a percentage, I hope you have a lot of other clients. It appears that Miss Minard hasn't made enough money to support herself, much less give you anything."

"Mrs. Londell," Em spoke up, "Skip is also my boyfriend, and—"

"Boyfriend?" Her voice dripped venom.

Suddenly a word I'd liked when Em had used it carried a very negative connotation. Like the term scumbag.

"Managing a career means managing a career, Emily. If an investment banker isn't getting you any kind of return, fire him. This is a results-oriented business. Sure, there is a lot of room for extras and second-tier actors, but there's no money being an extra. B-list talent is sidewalk spit in this town. That's why you hire people who are successful in their business to help you be successful in yours. I'm disappointed you are relying on lovers for your career." The lady's voice was ice cold. "Lovers are good for one thing, Emily Minard. Fucking. You need someone who gets the job done, not someone who is screwing you. And it appears Mr. Moore has been doing just that. Nothing personal, Mr. Moore."

Em nodded and I knew I was being sold down the river.

"We should discuss getting you a real manager, Emily. Because I don't deal well with amateurs." Her eyes focused on mine and she shot me daggers. "If you're serious about your profession, everyone around you has to be serious as well. If you're a professional, surround yourself with professionals. Got it?"

Em nodded, torpedoing my career as a manager. I wanted Juliana to be the killer in the worst way. The lady was a controlling, conniving bitch. Which, in this business, was probably the perfect agent.

"I will recommend two people, both males. I don't like it, but men in this industry," she glanced at me, "strong men, seem to carry the day. We women are still working our way up the hill."

We'd hit the mother lode. Juliana Londell was on board. We were in a position to learn a lot about Jason Londell's wife.

CHAPTER TWENTY-FIVE

The three of them marched into Kathy Bavely's office, and I sat in reception. I'd been unceremoniously fired. And although my fictitious feelings were hurt, I had a perfect opportunity. The secretary, whoever she was, had walked out the front door and never returned. I was alone with a lobby area, a main office area with a number of file cabinets, and an open door down the hall that led to Juliana's office. It was as if I'd been presented with the keys to the kingdom. The entire kingdom. It was all too perfect, as if someone was setting me up.

I heard Bavely's door close, and I was immediately on my feet. On the corner of the desk, as if it was planted just for me, was the proverbial gold-colored key. Way too good to be true. And I'd almost missed it, turning around when I'd passed the desk and shaking my head in disbelief. A simple handwritten tag attached by a thin metal ring said "office front."

It could only mean one thing, right?

Hesitating for a moment, I glanced back at the metal entrance door. I studied it for a moment, thinking everything was falling into place. Being in the security business, I was surprised that there wasn't an electronic-card entry. Just a key? I checked the walls beside the door and there was no sign of a security system. No pad, no subtle flashing panel. It would be an easy break-in.

But the Londell slash Bavely agency wasn't a cash business, and most burglars are looking for money. A computer, a printer, there wasn't much value in pawning anything they could steal. So your average thieves wouldn't find this office that attractive. Now me, I wasn't your average thief.

Glancing back at Bavely's office door, I slipped the key off the desk and into my pocket. Keys always went missing. I was proof of that. I misplaced my car key, apartment key, or some other key every other month. And if there were duplicates, you could always make another one. There was more than one office key, and no one would miss this one.

It was time to start scanning the metal cabinets for information. I just assumed that a high-end business like this relied on digital files. Why go to the expense, the storage, and the waste of dead trees by having thousands of paper trails when it could all be kept on a computer or stored on the cloud? It's probably why I wasn't yet successful in the business world. I didn't understand any of it. Old-school storage, but at least I didn't need a password to open the drawers.

The file drawers were labeled in alphabetical order, as would be expected. I scanned the letters and stopped when I came to *L*. Looking both ways, the front door of the office in my immediate view, I pulled open the drawer. Quickly looking for the name Londell, I found Jason's file. I flipped though the rather substantial bulk of the information and saw that it contained a number of contracts, reviews, photos, and more. The file was probably four- or five-inches thick. Everything seemed business-oriented, nothing personal. There were subfiles and more subfiles. His recent movies were listed, and I saw that he'd been on location in

Singapore just three months ago. Five weeks of exotic locations. Maybe Em was on to something regarding a new career.

I was impressed when I randomly opened the *D* drawer and saw Cameron Drew's name. Drew had a handful of Emmys to his name and even a Grammy somewhere in his past. I was surprised when I pulled open the *R*s. Eric Roster was on the list of clients along with Denise Richards, Charlie Sheen's ex. Juliana Londell seemed to represent big-name clients.

There was no sound coming from behind Kathy Bavely's heavy office door, and I stepped into Juliana Londell's office. Thick, maroon carpeting silenced the street noise, the ivory walls were adorned with Picasso-like art, with signatures of Georges Braque and Modigliani on the strange sketches and paintings. I had no idea who they were, but I never understood Picasso either. I actually took a course at Samuel and Davidson University in art appreciation, and after that class, I can truly say I have no appreciation for art.

This lady was about my age, but she had obviously climbed higher in the world than I had at this point. Original art, clients who made millions of dollars, and a relationship that was of celebrity, *People* magazine status. I hadn't even gotten my wings and Juliana Londell was already soaring.

Her laptop computer was open and on. I glanced at the screen, looked back into the hall, and told myself that Em's job was to keep the three of them tied up for as long as possible. If she could pull that off, giving me time to explore Mrs. Londell's files, Em deserved a show of her own. I was about to find out just how good her acting skills were.

I had no idea where to start. A million options were open to me, and I had maybe ten or fifteen minutes at the most. I could open up her Word documents and maybe there would be that threatening letter to Jason, but I didn't have time to find the password. And then I looked to the right of the desk. A Global four-drawer metal filing cabinet was within reaching distance. No letters or names appeared on the drawers, and I leaned over and pulled the first one open.

Auction Items. Apparently the Londells had given some of their furniture to an auction house. A walnut desk, whiskey cabinet—whatever that was—a maple dining table, and the list went on.

Auto Insurance. A policy for a Ford Focus, a Toyota Camry, and a Jeep Liberty were in the file. Gold. Another file listed a Lexus, a Porsche Boxster, and a Ferrari. They appeared to be personal policies, not licensed to the company. Damn. A Ferrari. She was my age for God's sake. A Ferrari?

And sure enough, when I found the *L* files, there was a paper file for *Life Insurance*. This was almost too easy.

Flipping through the few papers in the file, I saw it.

Jason Londell to Juliana Londell, Beneficiary. The policy had been taken out about four weeks after their marriage. It was for ten million dollars. Dear Jesus. Ten million dollars. Coupled with the value of his estate, this lady was worth a fortune. Close to one hundred million dollars if everything checked out. I got as far as face value when a stern female voice said, "What the hell do you think you're doing?"

CHAPTER TWENTY-SIX

Spinning around, I saw her, standing at the entrance doorway to reception. The secretary had a cell phone pressed tightly to her ear, obviously distraught about something. Thank God, her back was to me.

My heart doubled its speed as I stepped out of the office, moving quickly and quietly down the hallway, reaching the reception area just as she turned around.

Frowning, she nodded at me, walked to her desk, and pulled out her chair.

I took a deep breath.

"I've got to go," she barked into her cell. "She's not going to be happy, Steve. There's been a lot of effort on this end. You know that. You've had the auditions, but she can't make the results happen. You're responsible for the delivery and apparently the results are less than stellar." Very softly she finished by saying, "And when she's not happy, nobody is happy."

With that, she shoved the phone into her purse and sat down.

"These hotshot actors who don't have a prayer of moving to the big leagues, they pretend to own this town."

Glancing up at me, she said, "Are you a hotshot actor with no prayer? Because if you are—"

I shook my head.

"Where is Juliana?"

"In Kathy's office. With Emily."

"Oh, Emily? The hot blonde? They were discussing her earlier. She made quite an impression. She may have a prayer."

Everyone wanted a piece of Em. I couldn't blame them.

"Yeah. The hot blonde. Listen, uh—"

"Sue." She stared at her computer, then started typing as if I wasn't there. "Sue Waronker."

"Sue, so how long have you been working for Juliana?"

"A year." She never looked up. "Is that important to you? The length of my employment?"

"No, I just wondered." I had nowhere to go with that. Times like this, I didn't feel I was cut out to be a private investigator. I never was able to "couch" my questions. "She represents some pretty big clients."

"She *has*." Sue began typing fast.

"Has?"

"They come and go, Mr.—"

"Moore. Skip Moore."

"Okay, Chip." She finally finished, glancing up at me. "Actors change representation all the time. If an agent doesn't get them work on a regular basis or doesn't get them the right roles, they move on. If a movie bombs, the actor will lay blame on the agent for suggesting the role. If an agent doesn't tell them how wonderful they are every time they talk to them, if an agent doesn't literally kiss their ass, they go somewhere else. They're actors. They are not necessarily the most stable people on the planet. They are not necessarily the smartest people on the planet. You must be in the business. You know this."

Actors change representation all the time? I'd never heard

124

this. I assumed that if you had representation, you remained loyal because it couldn't be easy to be without someone championing your cause. Every time I questioned Emily's commitment, I didn't run for the next available set of arms.

"When J.L. left, well, the dynamics changed."

I'd never heard Jason referred to by his initials.

"Okay."

Glancing at Kathy Bavely's door, Sue spoke softly.

"Let me put it this way, although it's no concern of yours. She doesn't have the list she used to have."

"When," I hesitated, "J.L. was here?"

Sue Waronker nodded, a slight smile on her lips.

"There was somewhat of a mass exodus when he left."

"Really?"

"Mr. Rip? I told you, her clients are actors, and not the most stable people. If you are in the business, this should come as no surprise to you. Actors run here, they run there, trying to catch a trend, grabbing the coattails of the nearest superstar, hoping to catch lightning in a bottle. Throwing themselves at the latest movie trend and spending a fortune on plastic surgery! Right now we've got too many B-list actors. Juliana and Kathy are looking for *A-plus* candidates." She gave me a wry smile. "*A-plus* is hard to come by."

The Waronker lady was laying it all out there, telling me exactly how it all worked, and I decided to push a little harder.

"So, some of her clients left. Are you saying things are a little tough right now for the agency?"

That bemused smile again.

"Let's just say she is regrouping."

"So things need to be adjusted?"

"She's adjusting, along with Kathy Bavely. Thus, the interest in your lady friend. Possible *A-plus* talent."

After one day?

"So, obviously you need high-paid actors, gainfully employed, to make money in this business."

"Duh."

"Doesn't sound like a very secure business."

"Secure? Secure? You'd be surprised how many actors finish a role, and, with nothing in the works, immediately file for unemployment. Even some of the leads. One day you can be on top of the world, and the next day you're unemployed, and the critics don't even mention you." Sue turned back to her computer. "Secure? There is no such word here in Hollywood. From the stars to the grips, everyone is one day away from never having an industry paycheck again. Pretty scary."

"Still, a list of major players is—"

"I've learned one thing in my year in this business." Sue folded her arms across her chest and glared at me. "There are a handful of stars. The big shots, the Tom Cruises, the Bob De Niros, Jennifer Anistons, they make ninety percent of the movies and TV shows in this town. The rest of the people are supporting actors. That's all. Your girlfriend may get a job on this sitcom, but in a couple of months she'll be a has-been. An extra. Someone whose dreams have flown out the window. One percent of the talent in this town make ninety percent of the product and ninety percent of the money."

The office door opened, and Em was the first one out. A big smile covered her face and there was almost a swagger to her walk. Behind her, Bavely and Londell walked into the reception area.

"Three o'clock, Emily. And give them your best." Jason Londell's wife nodded to Emily, looking very businesslike and very sober. "We're counting on you for a good showing."

"I'll be there."

Em grabbed my arm, tugging on it, and she pulled me out of the building. I could feel the energy in her grasp.

"Skip, you won't believe it." She was squeezing my arm till it almost hurt.

"Em," I interrupted, "I found the policy." I should have listened to her but I had news of the case. She didn't.

"What?"

Her look was intense, eyes wide open, and lips pursed tightly.

"Skip, listen to me. I've got an audition. This afternoon. Honest to God. An audition for a TV show."

We'd stopped walking, and she was one inch from my face. I could smell peppermint from the gum she was chewing.

"It's for a guest shot on a sitcom." She was beaming. "The sister of a nerdy scientist. If I get the role, it could work into a full-time character. Full-time. Do you hear me, Skip?"

She was one inch away. I heard every word.

"I've got an audition!"

And I realized the reason we'd come here was no longer her main focus. Emily was about to become an American princess.

CHAPTER TWENTY-SEVEN

Henson Studios, on La Brea Avenue, is a historic complex that was the original Charlie Chaplin film headquarters. Since then, A&M records had headquartered there and now it's the home of the late Jim Henson's recording and film business. A storied past.

Walking four blocks from where we parked, I looked up and there was a statue of Kermit the Frog towering over the complex, complete with a bowler hat and cane. The statue was obviously a tribute to the late, great king of silent comedy, Charlie Chaplin. I remembered James, quoting the famous amphibian that stood guard over the storied studio.

"Try what? Plummeting? I suppose you could try it once."

Em studied me for a moment.

"I know, Kermit from *The Muppet Caper*. Skip, I know what you're thinking and you're right and wrong. I'm here to find out if Juliana Londell had anything to do with the—" she hesitated, "plummeting of her husband to his death. However, I've got an agent who actually wants me to try out for a part. What would you do? Think it over, Skip. What would you do?"

I honestly didn't know. Who was I kidding? I honestly *did* know. Without any talent at all, I'd still jump at the chance.

"Your agent is possibly a murderer."

"Your point is?"

"You're kidding, right?" I wiped sweat from my forehead. The humidity and heat and a four-block walk had taken something out of me. Em seemed as fresh as a daisy.

"What is your point, Skip?"

We all rationalize our lives. Our decisions are seldom based on anything other than self-indulgence.

"Skip, I get a little adventure, and I get very close to the suspect. It seems to me that it's a win-win situation."

"I think it's a stupid idea, Em. If we get caught, who knows what could happen." I actually had an idea of what might happen and it wasn't appealing.

"If, if she's the killer."

"You really want to do this, right?"

"Wish me luck, boyfriend."

It occurred to me that if she was successful in this audition, if she nailed the part in her professional acting debut, I might not be her boyfriend for much longer. There were no guarantees. I'd already been fired as her manager for not being up-to-snuff—one of my mother's favorite sayings—and now Em was about to go where I always imagined the casting-couch method still applied. This was something I hadn't anticipated. I hoped she didn't have to sleep with someone to get the part.

The guard at the gate asked her name, gave me a disapproving glance, and pointed to the main lobby.

As we walked the short distance to the entrance, Em told me what she'd learned from Kathy Bavely and Juliana Londell.

"The black-and-white *Adventures of Superman* show was filmed here," she said. "Some guy named George Reeves."

I'd never seen it.

"And *The Muppets*. Before Henson sold them."

I had seen *The Muppets*. Grew up with them.

"Some comedian named Red Skelton used to film his TV show here."

Obviously, long before my time.

"Mitch Miller's show and Juliana says that these people now produce some really great shows and—blah blah blah blah blah."

I wasn't listening. Things had taken a major turn, and I wasn't quite sure how to get back to the main theme. All of a sudden my girlfriend was trusting our murder suspect for career advice. It was absurd. How had things come to this?

Entering the lobby, I was immediately taken with the glass trophy case filled with crystal, gold, and silver awards for a variety of shows that Henson Studios had produced. The walls were adorned with gold records from Sergio Mendes and Brasil '66, Herb Alpert & the Tijuana Brass, We Five, The Carpenters, Captain and Tennille and other groups that my mom used to listen to. Obviously, lots of tunes had been recorded at A&M studios.

"Blah blah blah blah blah, Paul McCartney even recorded here," Em said. I'd tuned back in.

The lady at the front desk took Emily's name, questioned who I was, and then we took a seat on a soft, leather sofa next to three other girls about Em's age. I studied the award case, marveling at the history this studio had.

"Miss Minard?"

A chunky girl with acne and baggy jeans motioned to Em. We both stood up and the young lady held up her hand.

"Sir, just the lady. Miss," she consulted a clipboard in her hand, "Minard."

Sitting back down, I just shook my head. Em leaned down, smiled, and squeezed my hand.

"We're going to solve the murder, Skip. We really are. I know it's something we've got to concentrate on. But in the meantime—"

And she was gone.

I was on the West Coast. James was on the East. And Em was in La-La land. My down-to-earth girlfriend, always the grounded one, was now living a dream. And I was sitting on a buttery leather sofa, in a historic movie/recording studio, with three starlets waiting to see if the love of my life was going to be my partner or a silver-screen icon. Silver screen. Something else my mother referred to. Was Em going to be an actress or my girlfriend?

Twenty minutes passed and the heavyset girl appeared once more, calling out one of the three girls sitting next to me. The wanna-be actress giggled loudly, shook her long blonde hair, and followed the leader back down a hall. I'd seen her somewhere. A Tide detergent commercial?

Ten minutes passed and I was getting nervous. I'd lost Em before, for apparently no reason of my own, but this time, if she was successful in her sitcom audition, I was afraid we might be done forever. And believe me, I was never going to find another woman like Em.

"Skip."

I felt her hand on my shoulder.

"Em." I was shaking. Seriously.

"I nailed it."

"You got the part?"

"No guarantee."

"So—"

"I'll hear tomorrow. But I got a big nod from the producer."

"A nod?"

"The producer said, quote, 'You've pretty much hit every mark. I love your passion, your attitude, and what you bring to the character. We're probably going to ask you back for a second audition.'"

"Great."

"You don't sound sincere."

I didn't mean it. I had a hard time believing this was happening.

"We're here to do a job and we're spending someone else's money. If the situation were reversed—"

"Do I detect a note of jealousy?"

"No. Maybe. I don't know."

"Skip," she whispered, "we're undercover. Isn't this what we're supposed to be doing? Getting close to Juliana Londell?"

"I found out she has a rather sizable insurance policy on her late husband. That's what we were sent here to find out."

"We can learn more, Skip." Making the case for staying in this fantasy world. "Was she faithful? Is she trying to pull some sort of scam? Did she take part in the murder?"

"I'm not sure we can—"

"What?" Em's hushed voice was stern. "Solve the crime? If we go back to Miami, I don't think it furthers the cause, Skip. Ashley is not going to fund numerous trips to California, I'm pretty sure of that." She was talking in a soft voice, but every word was intense. "And what about Greg Handler? The camera guy?"

I'd almost forgotten about him.

"I'll get closer to Juliana." She wasn't giving up. "You find out what you can about her and try to find this Handler guy. And talk to James about the history of that other grip. There were four people on that scaffolding. Two are now dead. And we're not sure about another one."

She was right. She was wrong. But one thing was evident. There was a lot of information to gather.

"We're still working the case, Skip. It's just that I think I can be more effective in this capacity."

And I thought she was making an excuse to explore career opportunities. But she was right. There were things I could be doing while she was distracting the suspect. Still, I didn't want to be dating a television star, because I was pretty sure that I wouldn't be dating her long.

"So where does that leave *us*?"

Em stared straight ahead and took a deep breath.

"The producer, Martin Scott, wants to talk to me in an hour. Over coffee. He said he has some specific points he wants to address. And he wants Juliana there as well. He wants to talk to me, Skip. About the role, if it should be offered."

I ignored the ramifications. I concentrated on the fact that Juliana had been invited to the conference.

"So, she's out of the office."

"He called her from the audition. She's coming to the meeting."

"This meeting with Martin whoever?"

She caught my snarky tone.

"Scott. Martin Scott. If you're concerned, I'm pretty sure he's gay, Skip. Just settle down."

It was an ideal opportunity for me to go back and talk to the Waronker lady. Whether she'd talk to *me* was a different story.

"All right, Skip, I'm a little scared. Okay? Should I do a second audition? And what if I really got the gig? Do I carry this undercover thing that far?" Her insecurity was showing.

Squeezing my hand, she said, "But I really believe I could do this. And if I get the job, what do I tell Dad?"

It wasn't about Em being undercover. It went further than that, and she couldn't admit that. In a matter of hours, she'd bought into the hype. She was envisioning a possible future in show business.

"Em, I just don't know where that leads us. I'm your biggest fan, but there's a job here that needs to be done."

"They think I can act."

"You did a damn fine job of convincing them, granted, but

even your Screen Actor's Guild card is fake. We're frauds. Both of us. Pure fiction. We're playing a role. Don't you think someone will figure this out?"

She frowned, grabbing me by the elbow, and pulling me down the lot.

As we walked toward the gate, she talked.

"Skip, there are moments in life when you have to either bite the apple or throw it away."

"Now you're Eve?"

"Maybe. But here's an opportunity that may never present itself again."

"Damn, Em, you sound like James."

"And you buy into his schemes religiously, don't you?"

I did.

"An actress? Really?"

"I'm going for it, Skip. It's the best undercover role I'll ever play. Are you with me or not?"

I was always with her. But I was here to help solve a murder in Miami. Somehow I was going to have to do a balancing act. I didn't like Juliana Londell, and I suspected she may very well have had something to do with her husband's death. The lady was possibly a murderer, and now, now she was responsible for my girlfriend's career and future. What the hell was I supposed to do?

"By the way," she said.

"Yes?"

"You said you found the insurance policy. Unbelievable. In that short time I was in Bavely's office?"

"Yes."

"And you had time to look at it?"

"I did."

"How much does she stand to make? On top of a huge inheritance?"

"Ten million dollars."

"Ten million dollars?"

"Ten million dollars," I said.

"Ten million dollars," the words rolled off her tongue.

"The lady stands to make a lot of money, no question. It would be worth the effort to bump off someone you'd grown tired of, wouldn't you say?"

"Damn, Skip. That's a lot of money."

"Your dad's worth that, isn't he?" For some reason I'd always thought her father was worth multiple millions. It just came out, and I didn't really expect her to respond to the question.

"Like I said," she said, "that's a lot of money."

"You take your meeting. I'll go back to the office and talk to Sue Waronker. I don't think she likes me, but she gives me good information."

"Be careful."

"You too."

"We happy?" she asked.

It was one of my favorite lines from *Pulp Fiction*. I didn't answer.

CHAPTER TWENTY-EIGHT

James was less than sympathetic.

"Dude, she's always had this prima donna attitude. You've known that since high school. Your girlfriend is someone who thinks she should be a little higher up on the ladder than she is."

"What?" I knew what he was saying, but I wanted clarification.

"She believes she's better than we are."

Emily sleeps with me. I have no great job, no real future, and yet she lets me invade her space.

"That's not true, James."

"It is. You may choose not to believe it, but in one of your sane moments, you will realize your better half really believes she is your *better* half. Actually, she may be, but amigo, she is all about herself. Trust me on this, Skip."

"She is with me, James. How does that play if she thinks she's better than we are? How?"

I didn't want to hear it.

"Come on, man, secretly I like Em, but, Skip, she is so stuck on herself. Deep down you know that."

And I realized he was right. She'd always known she was destined for bigger and better things. I could tell from her demure demeanor, her smugness, her holier-than-thou attitude. But she hung out with me. She'd stuck with me for six years. So what did that say about the lady?

Now, Em was going for a career. A glamorous career that few people dream of. And here I was still stuck in a dead-end job. Selling security systems in Carol City, Florida, and working part time as a P.I.

I'd dropped the budding actress off at a coffee shop about two blocks from the studio, and I drove the rental back to Londell's office. Sue Waronker, the leggy brunette, was at her desk.

Glancing at the clock on the wall, she nodded at me.

"Almost closing time, Mr.—"

"Moore. Skip Moore."

"Yeah. What can I do for you?"

"Juliana had my girlfriend fire me."

She smiled and wrinkled her nose. "I heard. You are no longer a boyfriend-slash-manager."

"Is she always this take charge?"

"Juliana?" She laughed. "She's a ballbuster."

"I get the impression you aren't really that fond of her."

"She signs the check." Her voice carried a sarcastic smile.

I slumped into a chair across from the lady.

"Seriously, Chip."

"Skip."

"Doesn't matter. I've got work to do, and then I'm out of here. This was not an invitation for you to have a seat."

"She was married to Jason Londell." I wasn't about to leave.

"Duh."

"And he dumped her?"

"Oh, is that the story?" She wore a wide-eyed innocent look on her face. "Thanks for enlightening me."

"I don't know. It's what I heard."

"I don't understand how that could possibly be any of your business, but I believe I was a little closer to the situation."

"Oh?"

"Without giving away the exciting plot, let me reiterate what I said earlier. Juliana Londell is a ballbuster. She is a tough lady who doesn't let anyone get in her way. Anyone. Understand? Tell her that something can't be done, and she'll find a way to do it."

Suspicion confirmed. The agent dumped the actor.

"Let's take your bombshell blonde. Agent Kathy Bavely found her. Invited her back. Saw the potential. But the question is, who's representing your sweetheart to Henson Productions? Care to venture a guess? Who will guide her career and give her the auditions she needs? Huh?"

"Juliana?"

"Bingo, dude."

"So not only does she chew up men and spit them out, but she uses people to get what she wants."

"Hey, Flip."

"Skip." She was doing it deliberately.

"Dude, like I said, the lady signs my paycheck. I don't make much, but it's an income and I am not saying things like that about my employer."

I nodded. Receiving good information from someone who appeared to be extremely hostile.

"So Juliana left him for someone else?"

"That's above my pay grade, Kip."

I let it go.

"Another actor? Someone in the business? I'd really like to know. Do you have any idea?"

"You don't give up, do you? Why is this so important to you?" Looking up from her computer, she shot me a questioning look.

"Your boss just cost me some money. A commission. Seriously. She got me fired. And I'd like to know a little bit more about this lady."

"I've said all I'm going to say."

Sue Waronker stood up, rolled her chair back, and stepped away from the desk.

"Time to go, Rip."

Easing out of the chair, I said, "If you know anyone looking for a manager—"

"Oh, for God's sake. What kind of a manager are you? You can't hold on to the only client you had. Great manager you turned out to be. I'll be sure to recommend you to all my friends."

"Actually, I'm not that bad."

She laughed out loud, a throaty laugh that came from the chest.

"Not that bad? You overestimate your worth, Mr. Manager."

"No, Sue, you should be impressed."

"And why is that. Why should I be impressed?"

I smiled insincerely. "I landed a beautiful young actress who may have a very bright future, and I got her a leading talent agent. Not bad for my first time out, is it?"

I didn't point out that it had all happened pretty much in less than twenty-four hours.

CHAPTER TWENTY-NINE

I found Greg Handler's agent on a web search. I called, told the guy I was an independent filmmaker, and was working on a documentary about struggling independents in the industry. Like myself.

The agent gave me a phone number, and I was surprised when Handler answered. I didn't think it would be that easy.

"I'm between gigs right now," he said. "What did you have in mind?"

Explaining that I was strictly in an exploratory mode at the moment, I told him I just wanted to meet for a short time to give him my vision of this fantasy project and see if he was interested.

"Is there a paycheck involved?"

I assured him there was.

"Then, of course, I'm interested. Most of the time paychecks are few and far between in this racket."

I had a twinge of guilt. But only a twinge.

Surprisingly, he suggested a restaurant on La Brea Avenue across from Henson's studio, just a few doors down from where Em was being offered the role of a lifetime. I drove there getting a little more comfortable with the surroundings. After all, this really was a small town.

L.A. drivers lead the nation in the road-rage epidemic, and the maniac two cars back seemed to have invented it. In a black BMW sedan with tinted windows, a guy laid on the horn, swerving out into the opposite lane and careening around me, narrowly squeezing into the space between my rental and a white box truck. I braked and the Porsche behind me almost rear-ended my vehicle.

As the BMW cruised ahead, making another daredevil lane change, I saw an arm sticking out of the shiny black car, middle finger extended to someone. I'm not sure who had offended the driver.

Shaking, my hands gripping the wheel, I actually relished the driving in Miami. Crazy motorists, but not nearly the caliber of Los Angeles drivers. I've read since then that California road rage leads the nation in not only incidents but fatalities. Dear Lord, deliver me.

After arriving at the restaurant and settling into the booth, I smiled and nodded to the cinematographer. I was about to confront this guy and admit I'd lied to him on the phone. I wasn't sure how he would take that.

About thirty-five, trim, sandy-blond hair and a no-nonsense expression on his face, Greg Handler clasped his hands in front of him as he stared into my eyes.

"So what kind of film do you have in mind?"

The bleached blonde over-forty waitress with a skirt that was much too short brought me a Coke. Handler had ordered coffee and a ham sandwich.

"Have you ever worked in Miami?" I decided to get right to the point.

Leaning back in the booth, he studied me for a second.

"Is this about Jason Londell?"

"Yeah. I've got to be honest. I'm looking into his death, and—"

"You couldn't have told me that on the phone?"

"I wasn't sure you'd talk to me." I wasn't sure he would right now, but he didn't seem to be too upset.

Running a hand through his hair, he nodded.

"You know I've talked to the Miami cops. They almost sent someone here to check on me."

"I assumed." Finally the cops were exploring leads.

"And you know I didn't kill him."

"I assumed that as well."

"Then why the meeting?" He took a bite of the sandwich.

"Well, there are a lot of unanswered questions, and we've been hired by someone to get as much information as possible on what happened."

"So you're private?"

"I am."

"So there's no job and all I'm getting out of this is a cheap lunch?"

I saw a look of resignation on his face.

"Look, why you? Why did this guy who shot Londell pick your name? Greg Handler isn't a common name. I mean, no one would make that up, would they? Someone knew of you or your reputation."

"I have no idea why they picked me. Since Miami P.D. called, I've been thinking about it. There's a chance that I worked with the guy, and he decided to use my name, or maybe he just pointed to a page in the directory."

We'd had the same idea.

"Greg, do you know anyone who works on *Deadline Miami?* Actor, camera guy, grip?"

Sipping his coffee, he thought for a moment.

"I don't watch it, but doesn't Ashley Amber have a role on that show? You know, blonde and—"

"Yeah."

"I worked with her on a production. About four years ago. We did a couple episodes of some forgettable sitcom that got canceled. But I doubt if she would remember me. I don't know that she even knew anyone on that show. Nose-in-the-air kind of girl, am I right?"

I understood exactly what he was saying. She still didn't know my name. Kept calling me James. And James was just a guy she slept with. Wow. He'd actually done that.

"How do you know the show?" he asked.

"One of my partners and I are doing security for an outdoor set they've been using this past week. I was right there when Londell fell from the scaffolding, maybe twenty feet away when he hit the ground, and I swear to God I thought he took a deliberate dive. I did not figure that fall to be a murder."

"Deliberate dive? You thought it was—"

"Suicide."

"Must have been gruesome."

I kept my eyes wide open. If I closed them I would see the scene.

"You can't imagine."

"I've seen some weird shit in my line of work."

"Jerry Clemens is the other camera operator who was shooting the scaffolding scene. Do you know him?"

"Clemens?" Handler concentrated. "Doesn't ring a bell."

"I don't know that many people on the set. My job is to keep gawkers at bay. Occasionally, we drive the actors around, run a couple of errands, but I'm like you. I never watched the show."

Handler pushed half of the greasy sandwich away and finished his coffee.

"I don't exactly appreciate the way you got me here, but I'm curious about the situation. I'd like to know who felt they could use my name." Folding his hands under his chin, his elbows resting on the table, he stared at me intently for a moment. I finally had to look away.

"Do you think Ashley Amber could have anything to do with this?" he asked. "I mean, she may have remembered my name."

"Do you know her sister?"

"Sister? No. I'm sure I don't."

"Juliana Londell, Jason Londell's wife."

"No shit?"

"As I'm sitting here."

"She's a talent agent, right?"

"She is."

He smiled. "Maybe I'm glad I showed up. So there is a connection. Maybe the sister is involved and did remember working with me."

"Maybe. I don't know. I get the feeling that Hollywood is somewhat incestuous to begin with. Everyone supposedly sleeping with everyone else, jobs being handed out as favors—"

"I'm not saying you're wrong, but apparently I haven't been sleeping with the right people."

And I was reminded I might be sleeping with a future TV actress. It was all so very strange.

"The director for the episode, Randy Roberts, said something about sleeping with the right people. He said if he'd slept with the right people—"

"Roberts?" Handler interrupted.

"Randy Roberts. He's been directing this episode we're working on."

The waitress walked up to our table and, glancing up, I could see wrinkles around her eyes and a hint of a mustache on her upper lip.

"Anything else for you two?"

"No." I hesitated, not sure I should ask my next question. "Excuse me, ma'am, but were you ever an actress?" It was just a hunch. "Any television or movies? It just seems I've seen you before and—"

A long sigh and she squinted, her skin sharply creasing around dull, brown eyes. "Briefly. Back in the nineties. That was another life."

Dropping a check on my side of the table, she hurried away, and I was sorry I'd asked. She just had the look of someone who had come to town on a dream and, sadly, it had never materialized.

Handler watched her as she walked toward the kitchen.

"The town is full of them, Moore. More broken dreams in this small part of the world than anywhere else," he said with a nod, "in the universe."

I understood.

"You come to town, and if you're hot, everybody's going to make you a star. And if it turns out you're not star material, you're just another schlep laboring for minimum and calling your agent every other day asking why he's not working you."

"Life of a film actor is rough. I get it."

"No, no. Sure, the actor is taking it in the shorts, but it's not just the actor, okay? I'm not just talking about a film actor. Actor, director, grip, prop, makeup artist, camera guy. It's all the same."

I wasn't sure I wanted Em to have a broken dream. But I also wasn't sure I wanted a self-centered lady who had the world waiting at her beckon. Then I remembered, she believed in me, and that was important. Most of the time she gave me the support I needed, and *I* needed to believe in her.

Pulling out a ten dollar bill, I put it on the check. Not much money for an expense I could collect on, write off, and still get some useful information from. Little did I know how much information I would get.

"Thanks for not being too upset about my ruse."

"I've had meetings that were less fulfilling than this. In my line of work, you deal with a lot of kooks. You had a legitimate reason." Handler paused. "But, let me be perfectly honest."

"What?"

"You are still a kook."

"There's no such thing as a free lunch. You know that, right?"

"I've been around here long enough to understand."

We both stood up, and I reached across the booth to shake his hand.

"A last comment," he said. "I want you, or the cops, to catch whoever used my name. If I'm going to kill someone, *I* want to do it. Not someone who stole my identity. Understood?"

"Understood."

"By the way. Randy Roberts?"

"What about him?"

"That canceled sitcom I told you about. About four years ago. The one with Ashley Amber?"

"Yeah."

"I would bet money that Randy Roberts directed that. I am almost positive I worked with that guy and I think it was on that show."

"Seriously?"

"Pretty sure, man."

Coincidence? I thought.

"Hold on. You think Randy Roberts directed this canceled program?"

He totally surprised me.

"Roberts. Randy." Closing his eyes for a moment, he said, "This gig, it only lasted several episodes, but I think I remember the guy. Damn, the more I think about it the more I—"

"Try to remember, man. This could be very important."

"Okay, if memory serves, the guy used to drink coffee from an aluminum coffee mug. I think."

"Same guy."

"Okay, and it was rumored to be half liquor and half coffee. He hid it well, but I think the guy was drunk the entire time he was directing."

CHAPTER THIRTY

"So you know Randy?" This interview was going to be better than expected. I sat back down, and he followed my lead.

"Know Randy Roberts? No. I didn't know him. And I barely remember him. You work with a director, and if it's just one time, you don't really get a feel for the guy. Two times you know what he probably wants and the third time you sense beforehand what he's after. By then you are designing shots and setting up frames in anticipation of his demands."

The cinematographer held up his hands in front of his face and framed a camera angle, as if he was seeing me in his lens.

"It was the first time with Randy Roberts. I'm certain it was him. I remember I was not one hundred percent sure of what he wanted. The guy was kind of vague. Not a real strong communicator. And, like I said, I'm pretty certain he was lacing his coffee with something pretty strong. I feel certain that had something to do with his direction. The guy was a little loopy."

"But you remember him?"

"Yeah." Handler nodded. "Looking back, I guess I do. There's a team effort involved in shooting a movie or TV show. The director does a lot more than tell actors what to do. You may have seen it on your set in Miami. The director decides how to light the set. He is responsible for camera angles. He even makes design suggestions. So, even though we were together for maybe only two or three episodes, I do remember him. He was basically my boss. I took directions from him. It just took me a couple of minutes to process, you know?"

"Would he remember you?"

Handler seemed to be lost in a trance. His eyes glazed over, and he stared back at the rear of the restaurant.

"Mmm, I don't really know."

"You know who he was. Why wouldn't he remember you? I mean, you were his eyes, right? The camera guy?"

"This job tends to be somewhat of a blur. For everyone concerned. I mean, you do two weeks here, three months there, and six months somewhere else. Then a week, a day, or less in some other location." He paused, closing his eyes for a moment. "I've worked two hours before. And that was it." Handler smiled. "It's a blur of faces, personalities, and scenes."

I nodded, not really relating.

"Then, there's the layoff period. We nomads don't have the most steady jobs in the world. Directors are in the same boat. They move around like gypsies. My wife wishes I'd get a job that actually gave me steady work, you know? Would he remember me? Maybe. But there have been a lot of shows between then and now. A lot of camera guys, actors, lights, sets, and angles. So, maybe not."

There was a connection. Roberts and Handler had worked together. Ashley Amber and Handler had worked together. That was big news as far as I was concerned. A connection I hadn't had an hour ago.

"The more I think back, he was really a bad director. Just didn't know what the hell he wanted. I'm sure his drinking had something to do with that. I don't understand why producers hire people like that."

As his memory improved, I was hoping he'd call me with any updates.

"Again, I'm sorry I misled you with this interview, Greg, I really am. But help me out, man. Someone killed Jason Londell. Shot him. And they used your name to mask the killer. They used your name. Greg Handler. I understand you don't know why, but can you give it some serious thought, knowing that you've had history with at least two of the players? Maybe it was Roberts? Maybe Ashley? Let it gel and see if you have any other ideas."

"I'm unemployed. Got nothing else to do but think about it until my agent calls." He shook his head, and I could see he was processing it all in his head. It was a long shot, but I hoped he had some memories.

"I worked with Ashley Amber. And I'm sure I worked with Randy Roberts. Possibly other people on the show. It doesn't mean I know anything about them. I shoot the action. It's up to a director to get to know them and tell them what to do. How to react. The story has a plot. I don't design the plot, and I don't usually get close to the crew. I just help the narrative. But I'll work on it."

"If I e-mail you a list of the cast and crew, would you see if you recognize any of the others?"

"Of course. You'd think the Miami P.D. would have asked the same question, wouldn't you?"

"They didn't?"

"No. Wanted to know if I was the shooter. No beating around the bush. Straightforward. But I foiled their plan. Would have been easy if I'd been the camera guy, the shooter. But it wasn't to be.

"Good for you."

"Damn good."

"So, you had a cover story?"

"First of all I've never been to Miami in my life. And the second part was, I had an ironclad alibi."

"Just out of curiosity, what was the alibi?"

"I was filling out my unemployment papers at the office here in L.A. the day Jason Londell was killed. Those signed papers are on file and it's rock-solid evidence." Handler leaned back and smiled. "We'd just wrapped up a movie and, like I told you, I am out of a job."

"Okay, man, I'm sorry I bothered you. But you did get a lunch out of the deal."

"I forgot how greasy the sandwiches are in this place."

I smiled, hoping he'd get a job soon. He seemed like one of the good guys.

"You know, memories are strange. You don't have a recollection, then you start to force things, and pretty soon you remember a little bit about a situation."

"Yeah?"

"Then you're a little clearer on certain matters."

"What are you clear on?"

"The guy was drinking. Most of the time. And I kind of remember, early on the first episode, I said something to him about that."

"Really?"

"I'm sure I did. I just said something like, 'if you'd lay off the sauce, we might have a better idea of what you want.'"

"You go from not remembering him to this?"

"The mind is a funny thing."

"Tell me," I agreed. "You said that?"

"Something like that. He didn't respond is my recollection.

And as I said, we shot three episodes with him as the director and the show folded. It happens."

I thanked Handler and was sure that James and I had evidence in the bank and money well spent.

CHAPTER THIRTY-ONE

Pacing the sidewalk, I watched the entrance and exit to the coffee shop down the street. I didn't want Em's meeting to last too long, because I was certain the longer it went, the better her chance of a part.

Springsteen's "Born in the USA" blared from my pocket and I pulled out my phone.

"Skip?"

"Who did you think would answer?"

"You're in Hollywood, so who knows? Maybe Ben Affleck. Or The Rock."

"What's up?"

"We've got a situation. I thought you should know. Maybe not that serious, but a situation, nevertheless."

"James, we've got a situation here, too. I just had a conversation with Handler, the real camera guy. Of course he's not the shooter, we assumed that, but he worked with Randy Roberts on another project. Stranger than fiction. The one director we know and this guy has worked with him. And here's the interesting component. You'll never guess what actress played in that same project."

"Ashley Amber?"

My amazing roommate.

"Bingo, partner. I'm thinking Roberts should know who Handler is, and yet he apparently went along with the charade."

"You're saying the real Greg Handler has run camera for Randy Roberts, yet Roberts bought the fake guy with the same name? Maybe Roberts wasn't paying attention to the name. Guy was a one-time fill in. So Roberts didn't really care who the guy was as long as he could do the job."

James had a point. Possibly Roberts wasn't paying attention to the name.

"But Handler says the director has to know his camera guys. We've seen it on the set. James, they're a team. It seems to me he had to know that the *Deadline Miami* Greg Handler wasn't the real Greg Handler." I paused for a second. "And remember, Randy Roberts told me that Handler had been hired through Howell Video and Sound. Then Howell says he did not employ Greg Handler. So I'm guessing there's something very phony going on with Mr. Roberts."

"Give me time to digest, amigo."

"Handler says he would remember a director because that's his boss. He did remember Randy Roberts, but he gave Roberts a pass about remembering *him*. He made the claim that a lot of time has passed, and a lot of people have been involved in a lot of other projects. Still—"

"Still, what?"

"Well, as we talked, Handler remembered an incident. It seems that Roberts was in an alcoholic haze during most of the shoot, and Handler remembers saying something to him about trying to get off the booze so the directions would be clearer."

"Mmmmm."

"You said we've got another situation?"

"Our boss, Bill Purdue—"

Head of security.

"—called me. He wants to know how long my business partner, that being you, is going to be missing in action."

"James, I've got the flu, or whatever excuse we came up with. It's only been a couple of days. Someone can cover, can't they?"

"Listen to me, compadre. Clint Anders wants to know. Apparently, he asked Bill Purdue."

"Clint Anders? What the heck does he care if he's short one security guy? Until I ran into him under the scaffolding, he had no idea I even existed. That makes absolutely no sense."

"I don't know, Skip, but if Anders talks to Ashley Amber—"

"Yeah. They seemed to be somewhat chummy. What if she says I'm out here in California on her behalf?"

"Purdue didn't make any accusations. All he said was that Anders wanted to know when you were coming back."

I'd ventured close to the curb and wasn't paying much attention. Clint Anders was questioning my days off? The guy had a huge production he was in charge of and this was the last thing—

The black BMW was going at least forty miles an hour. I heard his roar three cars away and turned to look as he swerved into the second lane. I could swear it was the same car that cut me off earlier. The driver had thrust his hand out of the window and flipped the bird to someone behind him. Maybe me? Oh, shit. I froze, watching him now one car away as he aimed for the curb, increasing speed, and headed directly toward where I was standing.

As the sleek sports car approached the walkway, I jumped back, spun around, and took off running. As fast as I've ever run in my life. No strength conditioning, no workout schedule, yet I was making remarkable progress. Gulping oxygen, my lungs on fire, I achieved full speed, hoping the V-8 engine wouldn't keep up. Obviously, a very stupid wish.

The marauding machine followed, two wheels riding the sidewalk, scattering several people from their outdoor tables. Seeing an entrance to one of the eating establishments, I ducked in, hoping this focused driver wasn't being paid enough to run his automobile into a physical building.

He wasn't.

Gasping for air, I stared after him as the midnight-black car braked, took a hard right down the street, and disappeared from view. I wiped sweat from my forehead, shaking the entire time, and leaning against the inside wall of the restaurant I heard a squeaky little voice.

"What movie is this going to be in?"

Turning to my right, I saw her.

An older lady with khaki shorts, an I ❤ L.A. T-shirt, sunglasses, and a straw-brimmed hat was looking up at me, trying to remember what shows I'd been in.

"It's for—" I couldn't think of a movie or TV show. Not one. Concentrating, my hands shaking, I knew I had to sit down and come up with an answer. "*Harry's Law*. An episode of *Harry's Law*."

"With Kathy Bates?"

"Sure."

"Young man, you don't have to lie to me. That show was canceled several years ago."

I was the one who had almost been canceled.

Looking at me with disgust, she walked away, a pale straw bag almost her size swinging from her arm.

I fell into a seat by the window, staring at the street.

"Skip?"

Someone was calling my name, and the voice was coming

from my shaking right hand. I realized I had a death grip on my cell phone.

"James."

"What the hell is going on?"

"Somebody tried to run me over, man."

"What?"

"No shit."

"What happened?"

"Car came up on the sidewalk." It was hard to talk, breathing as heavily as I was. "Honest to God, James. I was outrunning a BMW."

"Why?"

"I have no idea, but this guy was gunning for me." I couldn't see who the driver was, but there was no denying his intention.

"About took out three or four other pedestrians, too."

"Guy for sure? Or girl?"

"I'm just assuming."

"Maybe you'd better get back to Miami."

"There are a couple more things we've got to do, James."

"Hey, if someone is chasing you with a car—"

James was right. I should have headed back to Miami. I should have gotten out of the P.I. business. I was much too young to put myself in harm's way. I was a little scared. And a little pissed off.

"Can't leave at this moment."

"What do you have to do that's so important? If someone is trying to kill you, we're too deep in this, Skip. Come on home."

All we were to do was check on Juliana Londell's life insurance policy and clear cameraman Greg Handler. That was it. And now Em was auditioning for a TV role, I'd been fired from a job I didn't even have, and someone was trying to kill me or scare the crap out of me.

Seeing Em exit the coffee shop, I walked outside the restaurant and waved. Juliana Londell was next, glancing up and squinting her eyes, frowning at me. The man following them had on a light-brown sweater and plaid green-and-yellow pants, like he'd walked out of an F. Scott Fitzgerald novel, or he was auditioning for the remake of *Caddyshack*.

"Skip, what is so important that you can't fly back?"

"We've got to make Em a star, James. It seems it's part of the plan."

He was silent on the other end.

CHAPTER THIRTY-TWO

As traumatic as the experience had been, I decided not to spring it on Em. I considered talking about it after she'd had a chance to discuss her experience at the coffee shop.

Actually, I thought we would go back to the motel, relax, and maybe take advantage of a one-bed situation. That wasn't to be. She started talking nonstop, and the contents of the meeting came pouring out.

"He thinks I've got talent, Skip. Martin Scott." She was babbling, obviously high on the situation. "Major potential."

Potential? I wasn't surprised. She was fresh, talented, fresh, good-looking, and did I mention fresh? I was starting to realize that Hollywood was all about new talent. Fresh, new talent. Someone who had the potential. Because almost all the other actors had been reduced to secondary roles. A handful of A-list actors, maybe thirty or forty of them, got the big roles. Everyone else was hanging on by a thread. And the representatives, the agents, managers, producers, and directors were all desperately looking for someone hot, someone fresh, who had the potential to be the next big A-list actor.

"He's done episodes of *Friends, Modern Family, Scrubs, The Big Bang Theory, Harry's Law*—"

The little old lady with the straw purse wouldn't be impressed. Half the shows had been canceled.

"Martin has decided I can do the guest shot." She squealed and grabbed my arm. "I got the part, Skip. I really got the part."

I was numb.

"And Martin is going to start fleshing out the character."

First name basis already. Martin.

"It may mean a continuing role. Isn't this exciting? Continuing role. I mean, we're here two days and even though I know we're working a case, I mean—"

Emily was almost always the grown-up in our relationship and here she was acting like a little girl. And I guess it was good to know she was aware of the reason we'd come to La-La Land. At this moment, I was aware of why it was often referred to as La-La Land. Em was a little La-La at the moment.

"And the fake card thing, I feel certain that Martin and Juliana can pull some strings when the time is right. Not that I'm going to tell them right now, I mean, but—"

I drove slowly back to Londell's office, keeping an eye on the rearview mirror and not saying anything. I fully expected to see the stalking shiny black BMW, but it didn't materialize.

"They want a new name, Skip. A new name? Apparently, they feel the name Emily Minard does not have a flow to it. It doesn't have the glamorous sound of a Hollywood star." She sounded somewhat annoyed.

I always was partial to that name. I even wrote a poem for English class when I was a sophomore in high school.

Emily Minard, if I were a bard, I'd write a greeting card, to tell you how much I love you.

I got a D for my effort. I thought I should have received an A for my originality. It didn't happen.

"You do know this can't lead to a happy conclusion, Em. We're dealing with a fake résumé, a fake union card, possibly a killer wife, a fake cameraman and—" I started to tell her about the car that almost wiped me out, but she cut me off.

"Just because she had a major policy on her husband, doesn't mean she's a murderer, Skip." Her tone had gone cold.

"Em—"

"You don't want this to happen, do you? It's not just the case. I know what this is about. You are afraid that if I do well, and this thing is a success, it will come between us."

"Listen to you. Will you take a second and just listen to what you're saying? Come on, Emily, this is make-believe. Fantasy. This is crazy talk."

"I go along with your ridiculous schemes. I put my life on the line. In the past, Mr. Moore, I have championed your causes on a regular basis, even when I thought they were the stupidest ideas in the world."

She had.

"And you won't grant me this one opportunity to do something I've secretly dreamed about my entire life?"

And again, I almost told her that I'd put my life on the line today, not even knowing why.

She shut down and didn't say another word to me until we arrived at Juliana's talent agency.

I parked half a block from the office in the closest spot I could find, and she jumped out and headed down the sidewalk. Juliana was giving her some paperwork to fill out. She promised she'd only be a minute.

As I sat there watching her walk away from me, two things happened.

A green Jag XKE pulled up in front of the office in a newly vacated spot, and the secretary Sue Waronker walked out of the office and headed toward my rental. As she reached the car, I rolled the window down.

"Hey, Sue."

Looking down, she made a sour face.

"The best manager in Hollywood, right?"

"The case could be made. It appears Em got the part."

Her expression was vacant.

"In the sitcom? The one Juliana had her read for? The blonde bombshell?" She looked totally bored. No excitement for a brand-new client.

I nodded. "By the way, who's Juliana's boyfriend? The one in the green Jag up there by the office?"

She shook her head. "What's with you?"

"I told you, your boss got me fired. You told me yourself that she is a real ballbuster. And I want to know more about her. Like who is she dating?"

Sighing, she glanced at the green sports car.

"Not that it's any business of yours, but the guy in the cool car," she ran her eyes over my cheap rental Chevy Aveo, "that's Rob Mason. You haven't heard of him? I'm surprised you two aren't old drinking buddies since you're in the same business. He manages some of the biggest new names in the industry. I would think he would be friends with you due to your huge successes." She gave me a broad smile, insincere at best.

I know sarcasm when I hear it.

"And he's dating Juliana Londell?"

"They seem to be friendly."

I smiled.

"Will there be anything else, Kip?"

"Yes. How long have they been seeing each other?" I had

162

nothing to lose, and the answer had value. If she gave me an answer—

She didn't. Rolling her brown eyes, she walked away.

"So, I saw you talking to the secretary. Flirting or getting information?"

"You know how much I flirt." Never. "I'm still working the case. Information, Em. Information."

"And you're suggesting I'm not working for information?" The bitterness had returned in her voice.

"Not suggesting," I said. "Stating the fact."

"For your information, Mr. Moore, Juliana started talking about a guy named Rob Mason. Another manager whom she seems to be very close to. Like maybe they were seeing each other."

I pointed to the car parked in front of Londell's office building.

"The guy with the green Jag who lip-locked her earlier today."

"Oh." She didn't sound surprised. "Anyway, since you've been fired—"

"You've got to rub that in, don't you?"

Em ignored my comment. "She said with her connection to this Mason guy, the sky was the limit as to my potential. So I'm thinking this might be a good deal for us. You and me."

"Us?"

"I think she wants to hook me up with Mason."

"Hook you up?" My voice rose.

"Agent and client, dumb ass. Let's not project things into this conversation that aren't there."

The turn of the conversation had taken me aback.

"I'll find out how long they've been dating," Em said. "If she was unfaithful to Jason then that fact might help us in the murder investigation."

Begrudgingly, I nodded. "Maybe this Martin Scott was right. Possibly you do have potential."

"You're just starting to realize that?"

"Damn, Em, I've been your biggest supporter since forever."

Pursing her pretty lips, she pouted and said, "I was always aware that I was able to get what I wanted, Skip. That was clear to me at an early stage in my life. But then I haven't wanted much. No huge-scale dreams. And Daddy had a job waiting for me after graduation that paid very well."

"So, all of a sudden someone else is interested, and you're willing to give up whatever you have to—"

"What do I have?"

"A pretty secure job with—"

"Daddy? He's sixty, Skip. Think about it. He's not going to do this forever. My father is going to retire if he doesn't run himself into the ground and die first. And then what? I run his business? I don't think so."

She was working herself up, and I knew better than to interrupt.

"I'm not an architect, I'm not a construction worker and, frankly, without my father, I couldn't and wouldn't do that job."

Up until this time, I thought she was set for life. It had never dawned on me that she was looking down the road.

"So what are you saying?"

"I need a new career."

"Really? Em, you're doing great right now." I hadn't found my first career yet. Still floundering.

"In your eyes, Skip. Not in the real world. And I'm not sure you play in the real world sometimes. Do you seriously believe that you and James are going to make a big career out of the P.I. thing?"

Honestly, I didn't. I was living James's dream, not mine.

"And even if you did, I'm not coming aboard full time. I don't want to be your girl Friday. I'm in your corner, boyfriend, but I have much higher goals for myself. And for you."

"What are they offering you?" I was afraid to even hear the amount.

"Three thousand dollars for one week." She gave me a weak smile. "If they continue the character, my manager will negotiate a new deal."

Three thousand for one week. I had a business degree. Still, it took a couple of seconds. A hundred fifty-six thousand dollars a year if she worked every week. I made about twenty-eight thousand a year. She was being offered five and one half times what I made. To be an actress. She was probably worth that, and more, but still—

"All right. I'm not exactly happy about this, but you've put up with some of my crazy ideas, so I'll get on board. You pursue the actress thing and keep Juliana distracted, and I'll keep bugging Sue Waronker, Kathy Bavely, and anyone else who can help us solve this case."

"Really?"

"Really, what?"

"You'll let me pursue this?"

"Let you?" I actually had a choice?

"Skip, thank you." She leaned over from the passenger seat and mashed her lips to mine. It was almost painful. Almost, but then the softness and sensuousness of the kiss set in.

Finally, she pulled away. Her dewy eyes, her flushed face made me wish for the sanctity of our motel room.

"I need you to be on my side. How can I do this without you?" Nodding her head, she said, "I want to solve the case. But put yourself in my position. Someone sees a value in your talent that you've never considered, and all of a sudden you want to explore that value. That talent. Well, I'm there, Skip. I want to see what the other side feels like. So far it feels really good."

So far, everything was an ego boost to my girlfriend.

Nodding back to her, I started the car. Potential was the furthest thing from my mind. Aside from my swim team coach in high school, I'd never had anyone who saw major potential in me. My life consisted of a disappearing father and a mother and sister who wrote me off years ago. Other than James and Em, I'd never met anyone who seriously had hope for me. No one.

And now I had a girlfriend who has just discovered she may be in line to be the next big thing. An American princess. Stranger things have happened. Sixteen-year-old Lana Turner skipped school one day and was discovered drinking a Coke at the Top Hat Café on Sunset Boulevard. Within a week, Zeppo Marx from the Marx Brothers had signed her to his agency and she became one of the biggest actresses in movie history. I know, I have a bottomless pit for useless movie trivia. Someday I needed to find a way to make that pit pay off.

CHAPTER THIRTY-THREE

In *The Postman Always Rings Twice*, Frank Chambers says to Cora Smith, the Lana Turner character, "With my brains and your looks, we could go places."

In our situation, it was Em's brains and Em's looks. Together, with her brains and her looks, *she* could go places. Sometimes she took me along, but I was kind of dragging down the potential.

I still didn't tell her about the BMW trying to run me over, and we drifted off to sleep never totally reconciling.

Waking up early, I realized it was eight o'clock already in sunny Miami. I walked into the fresh outside, listening to early birds, and called James.

"On the job, pard. Last night a carload of high school drunks jumped the curb and plowed into one of our sets. Guy on duty about got run over."

"Soundtrack of my life."

A car, jumping the curb, and trying to run pedestrians over.

"So, you're saying maybe yesterday in Los Angeles was an accident?"

"Not my call, amigo. You were there. If you think someone

was trying to kill you, then I'm with you. However, last night, three a.m., these five high school kids were potted, and they lost whatever control they had. No one was killed, but it was damned close. They didn't set out to destroy a set. They set out to have a good time, and it didn't end so well."

He was silent for a moment, and I considered the possibilities.

"I suppose it could have been an accident. Someone who was into excess. Drugs, alcohol, who knows?"

I knew better. That car was headed right for me and, if I'd been any slower, it would have hit me and thrown me half a mile.

"Maybe they were trying to scare me."

"It was what it was, Skip. I'm glad you're among the living. I had serious thoughts yesterday about what life would be without you. We've come too far and we've damned sure got a long journey ahead. You can't go now. Understand?"

"I'm not planning on going anywhere."

"How is the star?"

"Considering a name change. Emily Minard doesn't seem to make it for her management team."

"Liz Taylor is taken."

"*All* the good ones are taken. J Lo, Megan Fox, Amanda Seyfried, Blake Lively—" Some of my favorites.

"Honey Boo Boo," he responded.

I laughed out loud. Things had gotten a little too serious.

"Skip, when are you coming back?"

"I've got most of the information I need. Juliana has a ten-million-dollar policy on Jason, and she's dating some new guy named Rob Mason, a super manager."

"Ah. A new boyfriend."

"Or an old one that she kept secret."

"And he's going to help raise the kid?"

168

"I'm not privy to that kind of information, James. She doesn't confide in me. She doesn't even like me that well. And her secretary, Sue Waronker, who is giving me some good inside information, detests me. You know how it is. I've made somewhat of a reputation for myself."

"You always were the charmer in our duo."

"So where do we go from here? Juliana had motive and possibly was unfaithful. It's a far cry from anyone charging her with murder."

James was quiet for a moment, turning things over in his head.

"Well, I think it's clear. You need to break into that office when no one is there. Check the computer, Facebook account, Twitter, and tear the place apart. If you can find that she was screwing around on Jason before he died, she had a damned good reason to kill him. A ten-million-dollar insurance policy that may go south."

"And according to what you found out, a seventy-five-million-dollar reason, that being the supposed value of his estate."

"With that ten, it's eighty-five million dollars, Skip. Can you even fathom that? Eighty-five million?"

We both paused, savoring the dollar amount.

"And it all disappears if someone can prove she was unfaithful to him. Disappears. Do you believe that?"

"It all disappears, Skip, *if* someone can prove she helped kill him. I'm pretty sure that a murderer doesn't qualify for one dime. I'm right, right? And I know it was her. I just know it."

"She's a real bitch, James."

"I haven't met her, but everything I hear points in that direction."

Bright lights approached as traffic picked up along the boulevard. I gazed at the road that ran by our motel, hypnotized by the steady stream of cars. Even this early in the morning, Los Angeles commuters were out in droves, headlights beaming into the morning mist.

"Being a bitch, Skip, that in itself doesn't make her a killer." James sounded disappointed.

"No, but you can see the ruthlessness in her eyes. Her secretary pretty much told me the lady uses people very hard to get what she wants."

"Oh, and that's unusual in moviedom?"

"You're right, man. And I agree with you. I think she was involved. The more I see her, the more I think she's guilty. Of something."

"You willing to find out? You're going to have to make the effort to dig up that information."

I wasn't willing. I really didn't want to take that chance.

"Breaking and entering. That's got to be a serious offense, right?" I was just guessing out loud.

He chuckled. "Skip, it's a misdemeanor. I don't mean that it isn't illegal, but a misdemeanor. I looked it up online."

"You looked it up?"

"Well, I thought we might have to go there sooner or—"

"You thought *I'd* have to go there."

"Skip, I looked it up. If you do have to break in, it's not a severe sentence. That is, if they find you guilty."

"Not a felony?"

"No. It's not even breaking and entering. California doesn't have that crime on their books. It's burglary, vandalism, and something else. I forget. But all you're doing is looking for information. You're not walking out with a big-screen TV or anything of value. Unless you see something we can't live without."

I considered this. If we were going to get to the bottom of the crime, I needed to get more information, make copies of documents, and be sure that we had correct information.

"James, if you have any opportunity to talk to Em, don't mention this conversation. She's in somewhat of a vulnerable state."

"I get it."

"I'm not sure you do. I'm not sure I do. All of a sudden, she's getting this rush of attention, from actors, from agents, from managers. For some people that takes a lifetime. In this case, she's been here two days. I was thinking about this while she took a meeting with the producer of this sitcom she's auditioned for. Actually, they've already promised her the part. But I'm thinking of the term 'fresh meat.'"

"Wait a minute. She got the part?"

"They're already considering expanding the role."

"No shit?"

"No shit."

"You're not jerking me around?"

"No."

"This sounds impossible."

"Tell me about it. We made up her entire résumé. Other than a high school play, she's done nothing as an actress. You know it, I know it, but I'm starting to think she believes her own publicity. Not a good thing."

"Congratulations are in order."

"James! Did you hear me? Come on, man. They are going to figure it out. This isn't the real world here. Nothing is going to happen except they'll throw us out on our ear."

"Don't be too fast to discount this, Skip. I'm trying to fathom our Em—"

Our Em?

"—being the star of a television show. It's a done deal, right?"

"How do I know? I'm not in the business. She seems to think the casting is finished, and she is in the first episode."

"What did you mean by fresh meat?"

"Kind of how we referred to freshman girls in college. These people, agents, managers, producers, and directors, they lose interest in ninety-eight percent of the talent they represent almost as soon as they sign them."

"I'm not following, Tonto."

"There are a handful of stars. Leading characters. A handful. The others, they're bit players. If you're representing talent, you are only as good as the newest actor you rep. All these representatives, they're all looking for the next big thing. Actors on the B-list are a dime a dozen, but the newest sensation is a possible *A-list* commodity. Em is hot for the moment. Without a track record. If she really could pull this off and become successful, well, all bets are off. She is the current fresh meat."

Total silence on the other end, a continent away.

"James?"

"This is Emily Minard? From grade school, high school, college?"

"The same," I said.

"Let's just say, for imagination's sake, that she actually clicks."

"Clicks?" I was afraid of that term.

"Becomes an overnight sensation."

"Then what?" I asked.

"Better off not being involved in the Juliana Londell case. Am I right?"

He was.

"I really believe the Londell lady is guilty. But deep down, I guess I'm hoping that she's innocent. That way Em gets her shot, right?" I asked.

"Are you? Are you really hoping that Juliana is clear on this? You don't really want Em to become a celebrity, do you? You're afraid you'll lose her. I'm right, amigo. It's me, Skip. Come on."

I could have answered immediately, but James was my best friend and he already knew the answer. I didn't have to respond.

"Skip, get what you can and come back to Miami. If someone is trying to finish you off, if they're successful, then trying to solve this problem without you wouldn't be as much fun."

"One more attempt, James."

"On your life?"

"No. One more attempt to get as much information as possible from Juliana Londell. Then I'm coming back. I don't know about Em."

"My best to Em."

"Yeah. I'll pass that along."

"Skip, be careful. There are on-site cameras, security guards, and all kinds of other shit out there. You never know who's watching, dude."

"It's only a misdemeanor, James. Nothing to worry about."

And I was worried to death.

"Skip, one more thing you need to know."

"What?"

"Jason Londell—"

"The dead guy who started all of this."

"The same. They're shipping his body back tomorrow," James said.

"Autopsy is finally over?" I asked.

They had the cause of death.

"Yeah. And Clint Anders and Ashley Amber are flying out the next day for the funeral. I think Randy Roberts might go with them."

"Hmm, Anders knows Juliana, and if he sees me, recognizes me, or if Ashley tells him—"

"Can you get into that office and find what you need in the next forty-eight hours? Assuming it's there?"

"I don't have much choice, do I?" I already knew the answer.

"Em is the one who interviewed Anders. All of a sudden Clint Anders's interviewer is a rising star in his good friend's wife—Juliana Londell's—talent agency. And Emily is *supposed* to be a private investigator. All of a sudden she's an actress? How is that going to play?"

I had to pause and sort it out. Clint Anders's interviewer, Emily, is a rising star in his good friend's wife's talent agency. Contorted.

"Chances are they'll never run into each other." I wasn't so sure.

"God, I hope they give her a new name soon. At least he won't recognize something like Brandy Hall or Britin Haller."

"Where the hell did you get those names?"

"Went out with the two of them in college. You knew Brandy. Used to strip part time at the Gold Rush."

I did remember her. A lot of her.

"Man, she had some tricks that—well, why don't you suggest it to Em? I've never named a Hollywood star before."

"James, all we've got to do is get this information to Ashley Amber. Proof that there's a big insurance policy and proof that Juliana was unfaithful to Londell. Right?"

"That's all she asked for."

"I'll get it. As you said, if it's there. And hopefully before the Miami entourage shows up."

"Good luck, amigo. I'll hold the fort down here."

"Not much of a fort left, James. The army is moving west."

"If there's any skirmishes I have one piece of advice for you, comrade."

"What's that, James?"

"Keep your head down."

CHAPTER THIRTY-FOUR

Em wanted to see Universal City, but Juliana had her busy with new photographs, a superstar hairstylist, and a meeting one-on-one with the kisser who owned the emerald-green Jag, Rob Mason, manager to the stars. He kept her busy most of the day, and I was only comforted by the fact that I assumed Mason was dating Juliana Londell, so super manager was off the market.

I had been her manager just hours ago. But I applauded the fact that he had seen the potential, the talent. Or, at least, he'd taken advice from Juliana.

While Em was in meetings, I drove to Londell's office building, parking two blocks away and walking toward her office door, then approaching from the other direction. I looked up, down, and all around trying to ascertain if there were security cameras. I wasn't sure there weren't cameras in the tinted windows of the shops and offices leading up to her doorway, but there seemed to be nothing in the first block that was attached to the stucco building.

At the intersection of Delph and Hamersheid there was a traffic light and what appeared to be a camera above that light aimed directly at the approaching traffic. God help the person who jumped that light, even a fraction of a second before it changed. That person would pay dearly and have his driving record permanently charged. I'd heard that a lot of communities make hundreds of thousands of dollars off of those cameras.

In the next block there were two businesses that had cameras installed high up above their doorways. An attorney's office and an accountant. No big deal. These optical devices were aimed directly at the sidewalk. Pull up your jacket collar, duck your head so they don't get a clear view, and move quickly. I could do that.

Walking it twice, I noticed that the entrance to Londell and Bavely's office had two, count them, two cameras. One on the left side of the door, one on the right. What were they afraid of? Jealous lovers like me? These people were going to make Em a star and maybe they were afraid of me and others who would come in and cause a commotion. Maybe.

I walked the distance once again, attempting to view every camera in sight. I didn't think I'd missed any. But you never know.

When I was done, I realized that if someone viewed footage from this afternoon, they'd see me walking by those cameras four times. Stupid. But I could justify it. I'd gone down to the office, one pass, and walked back to my car. Pass two. Forgot something and had to walk back again, then back to the car.

I had a beer at a place down the street called Lonnie's, a liquor establishment that I'd call a saloon. Lonnie's had a camera outside and one on the inside as you entered. Looking for drunks spoiling for a fight.

Glancing beyond the antique bar, I saw there were at least two more cameras mounted above the hanging wine glasses and back-lit liquor bottles. In this high-tech world of surveillance there were probably cameras in the restrooms, too.

Damn, you couldn't get away with anything anymore. Cameras caught your action at every turn.

I walked over a weathered, worn, wooden floor, and it seemed the place was straight out of a western movie, complete with a long, distressed bar and a tender who wore an apron and a thick handlebar mustache. An old-fashioned player piano stood in the corner and automatically played what could only be described as honky-tonk, the keys clacking a rhythm of their own. A throwback in time.

The old guy behind the bar was busy polishing glasses as I sat down and ordered a beer, and he glanced up with a friendly grin, probably because I was the only customer in the entire place.

"Bar came from the set of *Rio Bravo*," he proudly proclaimed.

I shook my head. I knew a lot of movie trivia, but—

"John Wayne, Ricky Nelson, Dean Martin?"

James would have recognized it.

"Obviously you're too young. There's a great scene where Dean Martin shoots a guy on the balcony above the bar." He pointed up where there was no balcony. "Man tumbles over the balcony and lands on the floor and Dean, he looks at the bartender and cool as can be he says, 'I guess I'll take that drink now, Charlie.'" He paused. "You traveling through?"

"I am."

"Tourist?"

"No. Business."

"Gonna be some big doings in a couple of days in this town. Big even for Hollywood standards."

"What's happening?" I'd be gone, so I didn't really care.

"Funeral. Jason Londell, Academy Award winner, big movie star. You didn't hear? Got shot in Miami."

"No kidding?"

"Sad day for our town."

"Do they know who killed him?"

"Last I heard the fella disappeared. Londell was shooting a TV show and some guy just popped him. Apparently, he fell off a balcony, some catwalk and—"

I shuddered.

"Maybe an L.A. cameraman. Yeah, I think that's the rumor. Hell, I'll bet there'll be a movie about it in six months."

And again I was reminded. I'd been there, front and center. I'd watched the whole thing as he came crashing to the ground. And I had no idea he'd even been shot. What kind of P.I. was I? I played the scene back in my mind. Randy Roberts telling him to jump on the third take. Randy telling the camera crew to shoot on the second take just to get the angles right. Randy saying—

"Anyway, it'll be an event, I'll tell you what."

I stared down the length of the old western bar and thought about Dean Martin and the cowboy he'd killed. The guy tumbling from the balcony.

"I'll have that drink now, Charlie."

"I'm sorry, mister." He appeared confused. I joined in, not quite sure what I was missing.

"You want another?"

"No." I waved him off. "I'm good."

Finishing the beer, I thanked him for his time and information. I wanted to be there when my girlfriend was done with her meeting.

CHAPTER THIRTY-FIVE

Em was gushing as she ran out from Juliana's office.

"It's crazy, Skip. Rob already has some ideas about promotion, how a soft-spoken Miami girl walks into an agency and walks out a star. He seems to be very excited about the possibilities. This sitcom thing is huge. There's a lot of talk about how far it might go."

"Is he dating Juliana?"

"What? Rob? Yeah, pretty much."

"What does that mean?"

"I didn't come out and ask him. We saw them kissing, and I guess that's good enough for me."

"How long? How long were they dating before Jason was killed?"

"It's not something you can just come out and ask." She bristled. "He'd wonder what business it was of mine."

Rolling down her window, she turned away and took a deep breath.

"Smog, exhaust." Closing her eyes she said, "Whew, I wouldn't want to live here." She rolled the window back up.

"What do you mean you don't want to live here?" She wasn't making any sense. "So, you want to take over this town, own Hollywood, but live somewhere else? Is it possible to do that?"

"I'll have to ask my manager if I can still live in Miami and just fly out for jobs. Casting calls."

She looked at me and smiled.

"My manager."

"Who *isn't* your boyfriend."

"Not anymore. And, as of this moment, I'm not sleeping with my manager, either. Are you happy?"

"That's a good thing, Em."

We had an early dinner at In-N-Out Burger. I wasn't comfortable going to a bunch of the really high-end restaurants every night, and this sandwich shop was a California phenomenon. Billed as the best fast-food burger money could buy. As far as I was concerned, it didn't quite meet expectations. The burger was dry and pretty much tasteless. Maybe we *should* splurge our last couple of nights in town. I'd have to check with James and see what restaurants he'd recommend.

"What do we do tonight?" Emily asked, chomping on the beef patty and bun. The restaurant was crowded, so apparently a lot of people either liked the place or bought into the hype.

"I'm going to do a little evening work." I sucked on the straw in my Coke and considered my blatant lie to Emily. "Find out where the Londells live and do a little surveillance."

I surprised myself at the answer. I had no intention of telling Em what my real plans were this evening.

"You know, it might be a good idea if you don't come along," I said. "With this thing you've got going, being her client and all, we don't want to take a chance that someone would spot you."

"Driving by her house?"

"Don't want anyone thinking you're a stalker."

"Why do you need to see her home?"

I was making up the entire conversation. I had no idea why that would play into the situation.

"I don't know. But since I'm here, it seems like a good idea. It's part of that seventy-five-million-dollar estate, and I'd like to get a feel for that."

"So I'll hang out in the motel?"

"No. I had an idea."

I swear to God it just came to me. I was apparently in a groove, because the answer was abundantly clear.

"Today I stopped at a bar down the street from Juliana's office and talked to the bartender. He brought up Londell's funeral. Said it was one of the biggest events going on in Hollywood. So I started thinking—"

"Thinking what?"

I was winging this. Having no idea how to tie the idea into a coherent thought I just kept going, and remarkably it came out like this.

"What if you hit up a place where movie people hang out? I'm sure a lot of the conversation will be about Londell's death and funeral. And the place that seems to be absolutely Hollywood is the Chateau Marmont's bar. John Belushi died in bungalow number 3."

Belushi, the actor from *Saturday Night Live* and *The Blues Brothers* had overdosed there back in 1982.

"Oh, Chateau Marmont?" Her face lit up and she leaned in.

The place was an iconic landmark in Hollywood. Everyone who was anyone had stayed there, drunk there, eaten there, screwed there, or slept there.

"Lindsay Lohan, Adrian Grenier, Ashton Kutcher, Matthew McConaughey, I think they all visit the place. I could meet you later. You pick up some of the buzz and see what's being said."

"What if buzz isn't the only thing that gets picked up?"

Em was getting a little frisky, and while I normally applauded that attitude, I was concerned on a number of levels.

"I told you, I'll meet you later."

"Actually, it's a pretty good idea, Skip. You do your little drive-by and I'll visit the Chateau. I've always wanted to go there. This will be very interesting."

"If some guy in a godforsaken little bar down the block makes it the topic of his conversation, think about the rumors and stories that you could pick up at the Chateau? Everyone will be talking about it, and you've got a front row seat."

I felt pretty good about our plans. Except for my breaking and entering, which I didn't want her to know about until afterward. Other than that, we were doing exactly what we should be doing. Investigating.

Em bagged half her sandwich, reminding me that an actress had to watch her figure. We drove to the motel and she dolled up in a brand-new outfit from Rodeo Drive. After ten minutes with an iron and hair dryer, I was about to be impressed.

We'd checked no luggage, and yet this lady was coming up with unbelievable fashions that trended toward supermodel status.

"What do you think?" she asked.

Tight gold pants with spangled sandals that sported six-inch heels, a white tank top that pretty much advertised she wore no bra, and a gold chain that grazed the top of her breasts. I wanted to cancel all of our plans and just go to bed.

"You will rescue me from any predators?"

There was no way I could cut my mission short. She would be the hit of the evening, and if I didn't come back to save her, someone could take her away. So I had to get my information and get it fast.

Em was fresh meat. And it was my job to protect her.

"You're going to listen, right? See what the conversation is all about?"

"Exactly." She sounded glad to be back on board.

"Skip, if someone hits on me?"

"You're a big girl, Emily."

"I hate it when you call me that."

"Big girl?"

"Emily."

"Em, I hope you're kidding. But if some stranger hits on you, and you decide to act on that, then what the hell are we even doing together?"

"I *was* kidding. Skip, it was just an observation, okay?"

And I was in no position to make that kind of joke. No one was hitting on me.

CHAPTER THIRTY-SIX

I dropped Emily off at the door of the huge, larger-than-life white, castlelike building, with photographers lined up on both sides of the drive. Long lenses, wide lenses, Nikons, Canons, the paparazzi were out in force. Several flashes went off when she exited the Chevy, although why they thought a starlet would be escorted in a really cheap General Motors car I can't imagine. I assumed they didn't want to miss anything. As soon as she entered the building, they were on to the next car.

It was hard to believe I had actually encouraged her to visit the premier watering hole in L.A. by herself, but I figured she'd actually get some useful information. Also, she'd be occupied while I tried to get the evidence I needed from the files in the Londell-Bavely office. Without Em's knowledge.

Driving back down the winding road, something kept bothering me. Like a mosquito that you hear just before you fall asleep, but you can't see it. That irritating buzz, and you know sooner or later it's going to bite. There was something that James had said or something I was thinking during our conversation.

Maybe it was something that passed between me and the cameraman during our luncheon. Something pertinent to the murder. And I couldn't identify it. An idea, a word, a thought that kept eluding me.

You know how you have these thoughts and wake up in the middle of the night, shocked, totally wide-awake, realizing that you've come up with the answer. In the morning, if you remember that answer, you often question it. But that's me. Maybe most people don't have the same reaction.

I put it in the back of my mind as I pulled into a strip mall parking lot about two blocks from the agents' office. All the stores were dark.

Fifteen other cars were parked there as well, probably people who lived in the neighborhood. The pavement was well lit, and as long as the car owners were out by the time the stores opened, it was a perfect place to leave your vehicle. At least I hoped it was. All I needed was to get towed. Em on one end of town, me on the other, and no car. One hour. That's all I hoped for.

The moon was behind a cloud bank, the sky inky-black, but the neighborhood night lights were on, and a soft yellow mist cast eerie shadows as I walked down the sidewalk. More than once I recoiled, thinking someone or something was either following me or had jumped in front of me.

I'd pulled the collar up on my windbreaker and pulled the bill of my L.A. Rams cap low on my forehead. I felt like some pervert who was looking into people's windows or looking for a store to rob. If I was a cop on patrol, I'm sure I would pull me over and ask what I was doing. I didn't see any cop cars at the moment, but I was sure that could change.

Hunching my shoulders as I walked by two of the offices with cameras, I stopped one door down from Juliana's agency.

Reaching into my pocket, I felt the gold-colored key that I'd swiped from Sue Waronker's desk. I could only hope that it worked. I could only hope that no one had figured out I was the one who'd swiped it.

Two cameras, on either side of the door. There was no way to avoid them, but with collar up and cap down, it would be hard for them to prove who I was. And that was only if I got caught. My objective was to do such a professional job that no one would even suspect they'd been burglarized. Therefore, there would be no reason to check the video. Hey, I was in the security business. I knew how to do these things. I'd been doing this for a couple of years and I knew my business.

Maybe.

Head down, cap pulled low, I walked the seven steps to the door, inserted the key, and turned it, feeling the bolt move. Damn. It was that simple.

I turned the handle and pushed the door open.

A dim, emerald-colored night light highlighted the reception area with a ghostly glow, casting a green aura over the entire area. I froze, waiting for an invisible alarm system to telegraph its warning. As I suspected, there was none.

In the eerie light, I could see the file cabinets and the open doors to Juliana's and Kathy Bavely's offices. I had access. As long as no one had seen me enter. There are silent security systems and, although I hadn't seen any sign of one, you never know. I installed these systems for a living, and some of them were deceiving.

Pulling a small Maglite from my windbreaker, I turned it on and surveyed the area, hoping that no one outside would notice the wandering beam.

Being familiar with Londell's office, I walked in, opening the insurance file and pulling out the Jason Londell ten-million-dollar policy. I placed the four-page contract into the copy machine and pushed the copy button. Twenty seconds later the hum of the machine filled the office.

As the papers flowed from the machine, I went through the other company files, pulling contracts for several high-profile actors, authors, and producers like Jason Londell. Current or former clients, I wasn't sure which was which, I just wanted a sampling of the people she worked with.

Juliana's laptop was open on her desk, and I sat down and tried to enter a password. Her initials, the name of the agency, but nothing worked. I didn't know her birthday or wedding anniversary, so I gave up.

I did have the proof of an insurance policy. I had suspicion that she might have been unfaithful to Jason before he was killed. I'd done my job. But there was still something bothering me, I needed documentation bordering on proof. This was a personal quest. And, I'll admit, I was a little upset with the lady's attitude when she put me down in front of Em. I wanted some proof that she was a killer, but I was pretty certain I wouldn't find it. Still, I was determined to keep looking.

After rummaging through Juliana's files, I found nothing incriminating. I'd rifled her personal information and she was clean. I'd even looked under *M* for Rob Mason. There was nothing. Maybe on her computer, but I had no idea how to get into that.

I turned off the Maglite and, feeling a sense of defeat, shoved the copied pages into my jacket pocket. I glanced at my cell phone for the time and saw Em had been at Chateau Marmont for almost forty minutes. I wasn't thrilled with the idea of her being single there, but I also didn't want to leave the office until I had a chance to explore everything I could find.

As I headed toward the door, I turned around, and in the dim security light, I saw Bavely's office door, open and inviting. What would she have that Juliana didn't? Probably nothing.

I walked in, seeing a similar set of filing cabinets that lined the far wall of the small office. This was where Em had agreed to a pact with the devil. She'd walked out, full of optimism, confidence, and hope. And I'd done nothing since but try to dash her dreams and destroy her self-confidence. Partially because I didn't want her to succeed. Partially because it went against everything we were sent here to do. Prove that Juliana Londell was a culprit in the death of her husband.

The beam of light spread to a soft hue, and again I questioned whether anyone driving by could see that beam through the blind-covered windows. Shining the light on the file cabinets, I looked for the same information. Jason Londell. *M* for Rob Mason. There was nothing. I flashed my light on her computer and made the same play for password recognition.

Her initials didn't work. KB. The agency name didn't work. And then I remembered reading about the most popular passwords people use to protect their computers. Number one was *password*. Number two was 12345. Kathy was too smart for that, but on that list was *superman*. I concentrated on positive results and typed in *supergirl*. Nothing. Trying a play on words I keyed in *superagent*. Watching the screen I willed it open. The screen remained blank.

Any time you try to guess someone's password, it's a big gamble.

I walked into Londell's office, typed in *superagent*, and again, nothing. It was time to head back to the Chateau and see if Em had been led off to one of the suites or villas by some hot movie star or producer.

Ready to erase my entry on Juliana's computer, I stared at the word. Reaching down and touching the number one on her keyboard, I pushed enter one last time. *Superagent1*. The screen opened with a harpsichord sound, and I had full access to Juliana Londell's computer.

My smile spread from ear to ear, and I stared for a moment, not believing I'd actually pulled it off.

I was proud of myself, but decided to tempt fate. Walking out of the office, I entered Kathy Bavely's room. *Superagent* was still on the screen. I reached down and hit the number 2. *Superagent2*. Bingo. The screen opened and whatever was on that hard drive was mine.

CHAPTER THIRTY-SEVEN

Glancing at my phone, I saw I'd been inside for more than an hour. Although I didn't expect anyone coming in this late, every minute I was there presented a greater chance of being caught. I needed to do a quick scan of information on their computers, looking for the outside chance that there might be personal information involving Jason Londell or any infidelities that Juliana may have had.

Em was by herself and, while she was perfectly capable of dealing with almost any situation, I decided I should at least give her an update.

I pressed her number, and she answered the call on the third ring. The background noise reminded me of a huge crowd celebrating New Year's Eve. Somewhere in the distance I heard loud music and the shrill sound of several women screaming.

"Skip, this place is remarkable," Emily was yelling over the din.

"Are you getting information?"

I could hear her speaking to someone, her voice muffled as if she had her hand over the mouthpiece, and then she was back.

"What? I can't hear you. Skip?"

"Are you getting information?"

"Leonardo DiCaprio just talked to me for fifteen minutes. DiCaprio, Skip. Frigging Leonardo DiCaprio."

She'd been drinking. More than one or two.

"Unbelievable. I told him about the TV show. Do you know he got his big break on a sitcom? Something about *Growing Pains*." There was another pause, more talking off the phone, then, "He wished me luck. Do you believe that?"

"Does *he* have information on the case?" I found myself raising my own voice, more than a little pissed off.

"Of course not," she yelled back.

"So you're not getting anything useful? Right?"

"There are people talking about the murder. Yes. And the funeral. Lots of people are going. I'm listening, Skip, but useful? I'm not sure I'll find something useful. There's talk, okay?"

She couldn't just walk around asking people what they knew, like she was a detective. It didn't work that way.

"When are you coming back?" The noise was even louder.

Fifteen or twenty minutes going through the computers and depending upon traffic another thirty minutes.

"At least another hour. Maybe you can run into Ben Affleck or Lindsay Lohan. See if they can help with our Londell investigation." I was pissed, but I knew it had nothing to do with her being there. It was simply my inability to cope with the situation.

"What? Skip, I can barely hear you. Come on in when you get back, and I should be here."

Apparently my dripping sarcasm was lost on the new starlet. I was on my own courting a possible misdemeanor charge, and my girlfriend was hanging with the elite celebrity crowd.

Turning back to Bavely's computer, I stared at the screen. Em had said, "I *should* be here?" As if she might not be there when I returned. What the hell did that mean? Where would she go?

Kathy Bavely's icons were well organized, and the one that jumped out at me was in the middle of those colorful tiles.

J's Schedule.

I clicked on it and the screen opened immediately. A calendar appeared and every box for the month was filled with Juliana's appointments. I couldn't tell if Juliana had added them, or if this was Kathy Bavely's way of keeping track of *superagent1*, but if this was to be believed, Londell had not left the state. There was no way she had gone to Miami. Every day for the last twelve months seemed to be full of activities for *superagent1*. That in itself didn't absolve her from any guilt, but we couldn't—*I* couldn't—place her at the scene of the crime.

And then, working backward, there were meetings with clients, and initials that had me guessing. The two letters that popped up before the murder and after didn't confuse me at all.

R.M. lunch.

R.M. dinner.

R.M. dropped her off.

Rob Mason was obviously more than a manager of talent. He and Juliana seemed to have been in a relationship that possibly had started before the murder. Maybe two or three weeks before.

I rifled through the preceding month and R.M. was off the map. Had she found this guy two weeks before Jason was killed and decided to have an affair? Then killed her husband so he wouldn't find out and cancel her seventy-five-million-dollar inheritance? That didn't seem to add up.

Going a little deeper, I saw the initials C.A.

C.A. dinner.

C.A. stopped in ten a.m.

C.A. took her to lunch.

C.A. dropped her off, early morning.

I only knew one C.A. in Juliana's circle. Clint Anders. Jason Londell's good friend and his last employer and producer.

The attention to lunch appointments, early drop offs, and dinner engagements led me to believe that Kathy Bavely was keeping tabs on her partner, or in this case, apparently her boss. I didn't know why, but she was keeping a personal log, spying on Juliana's personal affairs. It certainly seemed that way. Maybe it was because Juliana was all about stealing Kathy's clients. Clients like Em.

CHAPTER THIRTY-EIGHT

There was an underlying tension between the two ladies, that was a given, but I had to wonder why she was logging the meetings that Londell had with these two guys, Clint Anders and Rob Mason.

Scanning the calendar, I kept checking out the months preceding Londell's death. Three months back she had blocked out a section of the calendar with J.L. SP. Every day. I concentrated, thinking about what those initials meant. And then it hit me. Jason had been in Singapore. That must have been her abbreviation. SP. Singapore. And every day he was gone, Juliana apparently had an appointment with someone else. J.L. SP. Jason Londell, Singapore.

I also noticed that in some of the boxes was the comment, "See B.T."

I had no idea. Scanning through the icons, I saw nothing about B.T.

And for about two weeks C.A. and B.T. appeared together, as if there was a three-way meeting between Juliana, Clint, and B.T.

I Googled the initials B.T. and a broadband website and a music site came up, but nothing seeming to have a correlation. B.T. It could be anything. My guess was it was another guy who had some relationship with Juliana.

The other calendar that intrigued me was one that showed dates and four initials. The time frame started about three months ago. This one was titled J.L., but simply had four initials in each day part. Ph A A. Sometimes the initials appeared a couple of times in one day, but more often it was every three or four days. Ph A A. There were numerous mentions. Not one word of what it meant. As if to just remind her that the day included Ph A A.

Ph A A. I didn't have a clue. I put it in my mind and kept reminding myself it was there. Sooner or later, something would come up. Ph A A.

Making sure I erased whatever trace there was that I had been on her site, I left Bavely's office, after rubbing the windbreaker sleeve over the keyboard in case someone checked for fingerprints.

I walked into Juliana's office and smiled when I saw the keyboard lit up. *Superagent1*. I now was pretty sure that Kathy Bavely was pimping Juliana Londell. She knew that Londell's password was *superagent1* so she assumed the password *superagent2* without Juliana's knowledge and was keeping some sort of a scorecard.

Scanning the icons, there was no calendar for *superagent1*. But there was an icon for B.T.

I clicked it and the name Betsy Timmermeister flashed on the screen. Bingo. A spreadsheet icon appeared and I clicked on it.

Dates, dollar amounts, values on cars, buildings, houses, boats, bank accounts, investments. Row after row of numbers. I'm certain my mouth dropped open. It was a huge amount of information to absorb.

Thousands of dollars. Hundreds of thousands of dollars. Hundreds and hundreds of thousands. Probably millions. I'd never seen so many zeros on a spreadsheet before, even in my business classes at Samuel and Davidson University. I would bet some Fortune 500 companies didn't have this kind of a balance sheet. My eyes were wide open as I stared at the figures.

With just a brief glance, I realized I had the Londell fortune in my grasp. Betsy Timmermeister was some sort of financial guru who kept at least seventy-five million dollars organized for Jason and Juliana Londell. And if I had to bet, I'm sure the ten-million-dollar life insurance policy was included as well.

It would take an hour to pore through the entire spreadsheet, and I couldn't afford to be in the office that long. I hit the print button and heard the hum of her machine. I hoped that she didn't have the software to check her computer to see what had been printed. I'm sure most people don't. Anyway, this office was too small for anyone to care about paper usage. Who would suspect that an ex-manager of a budding starlet, who'd been fired from his job, was stealing Juliana Londell's financial report?

And remembering that I'd been fired from a manager's position that I never really had made me feel better about copying what turned out to be twenty pages of financial reports. I couldn't even imagine going through the numbers.

Quickly scanning Juliana's e-mail, I keyed in Jason Londell's name. She'd kept an impressive list of messages to and from the actor. Hundreds. Too many to print, and I didn't have time to see if there were threatening e-mails.

Turning off the computer, wiping the keyboard, I used the Maglite to find my way to the door. I hunched my shoulders, buried my cap-covered head, and locked the door behind me, making sure to hide my face at all times from the camera.

As I walked away, I put my hand inside my windbreaker,

touching the papers stuck in my waistband. I didn't know what it was going to prove, but it sure was going to make some interesting reading.

One hour and twenty minutes later, I pulled up in front of Chateau Marmont. The valet guy was at my door in an instant, and I watched him as his eyes scanned my vehicle. In the bright entrance lights, I could see the look of disdain on his face.

"Valet, sir?"

What the hell.

"Yes. And please, make sure not to park too close to another car. I don't want to ding this vehicle."

He smirked, as if he understood the joke.

Stepping out of the car, I watched the paparazzi lined up on the sidewalk. Not a one of them even gave me a glance.

I walked in, looking to my left and right, trying to separate the beautiful Em from the throng of crazy people who packed the room.

I couldn't find her, but I knew I could use a beverage, so I walked to the crowded bar and stared halfway down at one of the attractive young girls slinging drinks. She frowned at me and kept pouring and mixing. Obviously, my captivating charm didn't work on her. The muscular male in the black T-shirt and stubbly beard noticed my state and stepped in front of me, asking me what would be my pleasure. So, I could get the big guy's attention but—

With a beer in my hand, I walked away from the bar and started searching for Em.

I was invisible. No one stepped out of my way, and no one glanced at me. A ghost, walking through a throng of involved people. Involved in their own little worlds, their own conversations, their own cliques, and ignoring the man with a history of seventy-five million dollars in his possession. No, I didn't have the seventy-five million dollars. But I could control the fate of that money. I had names, account numbers, dollar figures. I probably had information that could stop the flow of assets to Juliana Londell. You never know.

Feeling somewhat empowered, I made it through one pass of the room. I didn't see any noticeable celebs, even though I expected to run into one at every table. If there were celebrities, I was blind to them.

"Skip."

I felt her smooth arms around my neck and I knew she'd found *me*, not the other way around.

"Where have you been? I was almost abducted by Ashton Kutcher." She giggled and I said nothing. My girlfriend was having way too much fun, and I was not feeling like fun at this moment. I'd had a remarkable stroke of luck at Juliana's office and I wasn't ready to get into party mode.

"Come on, Skip." Again, the giggle. "I could get used to this. Lots of hot movie people coming on to me and—"

She was drunk. Her hands drifted from my neck to my chest and I knew I had to make a judgment call.

"Look, Em, I don't know what's happened here, but I need to go back to the motel to organize—" I stopped. I hadn't told her what I was doing.

"Organize what? What have you been up to? Have you been a naughty boy? Mmmm?"

"Sort of."

"What? Tell me."

"In the car. I'll surprise you."

"This guy giving you a tough time, Miss?"

Out of the blue a hired thug stared down at me.

"No, no," she pleaded. "This is my boyfriend. You are my boyfriend, right?" she asked.

"Yeah."

"Gonna disappoint a lot of guys here tonight." The hard-ass guy looked down at me with a smirk on his face.

"That's the breaks," I said.

He appraised me from head to toe, shook his head in disgust, and walked away. If I'd had a couple of drinks I'd have hit him. No, I wouldn't have. He was much bigger than I was.

"Seriously, Em. I've got some good stuff to tell you. I think you'll be very interested in what I've got."

"Do we have to go? The party is just getting started. And Skip, you won't believe this, but I haven't paid for one drink tonight. Not one."

I believed it.

"We have to go."

Pouting, she put her glass on a table and her hand in mine. We walked toward the door, and I wondered if this would be one of her frequent haunts if she ever made the big time.

The minute we hit the drive, flashbulbs started popping.

CHAPTER THIRTY-NINE

"Em, I broke into Juliana's office."

"You what?"

"I needed real stuff. Copies of the insurance policy, information on her manager boyfriend, financial reports."

"Skip, you could mess up my chances to—"

"*Your* chances? Really?"

I had to remember that she'd been drinking, but Em was over the top, even for someone who was three sheets to the wind.

"I could have been arrested for robbery. For robbery, Em. That would mess up *my* chances."

"I'm sorry. I just wish you'd told me what you were doing." That little-girl voice that she uses when she's had one or two too many. And she'd had at least one or two too many.

"I didn't want to implicate you."

"Oh, that's sweet."

I didn't tell her the real reason. I didn't want her talking me out of my evening adventure. And she would have tried.

"Okay, Skip. Tell me what you found."

As I drove back to the motel, I explained what I'd seen and copied. She'd nod, give me an encouraging "way to go," then start talking about someone she saw at the Chateau or an exotic drink that seemed to be wildly popular on the West Coast. Someone had introduced her to a screenwriter and she'd met a makeup artist. On and on.

Finally, I gave up and she fell silent. When we got to our room, she was in bed in five minutes and seconds later dead to the world.

Sitting at the small desk, I pulled out the life insurance policy from State Commonwealth and glanced over page one. Lots of legal jargon, but one thing stood out very clearly. The policy would not pay off if the insured committed suicide within the first two years.

So, if Juliana was behind the murder, she couldn't make it look like a suicide. It would hold up the payment.

There was also a clause that said in the first two years of the policy, any accidental death was subject to strict review by the insurance company. Suicide and accidental death were off the table. Murder, apparently, was acceptable.

I had seen no record of a payout in her files, so State Commonwealth was apparently still investigating the death. I found out later that is called a contestability period. Ten million bucks. The insurance people didn't want to part with that kind of money until they'd checked out every detail.

The annual premium on the policy was staggering. Five grand a month, sixty thousand dollars a year. It would take me over two years to make that much and for him it was just a policy premium.

And another thing that came to the surface. This insurance company was covering their own ass big time. Every other line in the contract had a "however." There seemed to be loopholes for loopholes. The company would pay if this happened, *however*. The policy says that the insurance company should pay under these conditions, *however*. I never had seen so may *howevers* in a document. To be honest, I had never seen that many documents.

Then I pulled out the B.T. documents. Betsy Timmermeister had outlined everything in great detail. My God, there were real estate holdings in Hawaii and St. Barts, property in the heart of Manhattan and in San Francisco. A couple of million dollars in gold bullion and an interest in a silver mine in Brazil. The two of them owned two vineyards in New Zealand and a mansion in Amagansett on Long Island along with a publishing company and God knows what else.

It was fascinating. A collection of racing boats was valued at three million dollars, and an art collection was listed at two million. The guy even owned part of a brothel in Nevada. Who owns a whorehouse? It was crazy.

There could easily have been seventy-five million dollars on the books. This fortune was huge. And the widow Londell was the sole beneficiary. It said so on the spreadsheet. Supposedly this was all hers—unless she was unfaithful. I needed a copy of that prenup agreement. I needed to see exactly what the terms of unfaithful were.

How did someone amass this kind of portfolio? The guy was what, thirty-five years old? I was pretty sure that in ten years I wasn't going to be close to this kind of money. But Em, sleeping ten feet from me, she'd already landed a role on a new television show and if her career took off, who knew?

I hadn't looked for the prenup when I was searching Juliana's files. Damn, it was too late to go back now. What did the document demand? That she be caught in bed with somebody? That she'd shared incriminating text messages? Maybe there were inappropriate photos that were shared? Who was going to prove she was sleeping with someone when Jason was away? Or would

Jason's friends spy on her? I had no idea how something like this worked.

As I watched her, Em rolled over and opened one eye.

"I got some good stuff," I said.

"So did I," I thought she mumbled.

"What did you say?"

"So. Did. I."

I couldn't help but smile.

"Yeah. I know. You told me in the car."

Slowly opening the other eye, she showed me a sleepy grin.

"You don't think that I'm working on the case, do you? You don't trust me, Skip. You aren't sure I'm helping you." Her words ran together.

"Em, you're doing what you have to do. I get it."

"Okay." She closed her eyes and was quiet.

"Em, you still awake?"

"Mmm. Mmm."

"Londell has at least seventy, seventy-five million dollars in his estate. I've got a list right here. It's amazing how much this guy made in his short lifetime."

"Mmm."

"Did you hear me? Maybe seventy-five million."

"Mmm. Mmm."

"So, let's say you do become an actress. Let's say you do hit your stride in the next two years. It's a long shot, but there's some serious money to be made."

"Uh-huh."

"And Juliana stands to inherit all of Jason's money. Plus a ten-million-dollar life insurance policy. Think about that, Em. That power-hungry agent of yours is set for life. For her life and maybe one hundred other lives."

Her eyes were open again, and she nodded.

"She won't need you, or anyone. Ever again."

"I'll be a big star. I won't need her."

"Yeah. But she only gets the money if she passes the prenup conditions," I said. "Prenup."

"I'm a little woozy, okay? Too many martunees." She giggled.

"Yeah, well, go to sleep, and we'll talk in the morning."

"Skip?"

"Yeah."

"I was working the case."

"Sure, Em."

"I met a guy tonight."

"You apparently met a lot of guys tonight."

"No, no. I did, but this guy, we started talking. Well, I told him about the comedy and all and—"

"And, what?"

"He asked who my agent was."

"Wanted to offer you another role?"

She was quiet.

"Sweetheart, you haven't started on your first one yet."

"Turns out he knows Juliana," she said.

"A lot of people do."

"He worked for her husband."

"Gardener? Chauffeur? Chef? With Jason Londell's money the guy could afford a nice staff."

"Investigator."

"Yeah?" I was intrigued.

"It was his job to keep tabs on Juliana."

"What?"

"He was following my agent. It was his job," she paused and hiccupped, "his job to follow her. Pretty interesting, right?"

"He told you this?"

"Jason hired this guy to see if Juliana was fooling around on him."

"You met this guy, and he shared that kind of information?"

Some perv with a camera peeping into Juliana's bedroom window. And I suddenly realized it was exactly like James and me. Peering into people's private lives.

"He doesn't like her a whole lot."

"Em, what did he say?"

"He's pretty sure she was unfaithful from the beginning."

I hadn't dreamed sending Em to the Chateau would end up like this.

"Wow. You actually met this guy, and he offered up this information?"

"It's a small town. He said so himself. Incestuous," she mangled the word and laughed, "is how he put it. It just happened, Skip. I was telling him about my audition and it all came out."

"Wow." I repeated myself. "Wow." It was a pretty amazing story. "Does he know what the prenup says?"

"Oh, he knows," she said. "Jason shared everything with him. I'll call Gene tomorrow and have him make us a copy."

"Gene?"

"Gene something."

"He'd do that? Really?" Oh, my God. A copy. That alone was worth the price of admission.

"His card is in my purse. Two things going for me, Skip." She was slurring her words.

"What are those two things?" I couldn't believe our luck.

"He really doesn't like Juliana. Said she was a witch from hell and even gave hell a bad name." She giggled again.

I had to remember that. A witch who gave hell a bad name.

"And what's the second thing going for you?"

"He really liked me."

"Yeah?"

"Asked me out tomorrow night."

With that she rolled over, and in a minute, she was lightly snoring.

CHAPTER FORTY

"So now we have more interviews, more time on the clock, and I suppose we can bill Ashley more money," I said. Emily just sat on the motel bed looking glum. "I think we have to talk to Betsy Timmermeister and Gene somebody." Everything was getting more complicated. James would love it.

"Milner. Gene Milner. Says so on the card," she croaked, pointing to the card in front of her. "I kept it in case." She rocked back and forth, holding her pretty head in her hands.

"Gene Milner, P.I. Are you attracted to P.I.s?"

"Skip."

It was nine a.m. and my girlfriend was obviously hungover. Big-time.

"Okay. This guy," I referred to the card again, "Gene Milner, the guy who asked you out tonight, he was working for Jason Londell?"

"Said so."

Perched on the edge of the bed in a beige bra and panties, she sipped her cup of bitter coffee, courtesy of the cheap coffeemaker and cheaper coffee pack provided by the really cheap motel.

"So, we really do need to talk to this Milner. And, find a way to get that prenup so we can study it."

"He'll give it to me. All I've got to do is call him. If he thinks I've got something on Juliana, he'll be all over it."

And all over you, I thought.

"You did tell him you weren't available for that date, right?"

She rolled her eyes and shook her head in disgust.

"Besides getting the agreement, what am I going to ask him?" She avoided eye contact.

"He was trying to get incriminating evidence on Juliana. See what he got. It sounds like he's willing to share."

"If I'm willing to share," she said.

"We don't have much to share. I'm sure that he had access to Londell's portfolio while Jason was alive. We haven't got much else."

"And what about this Betsy Timmermeister?" She stumbled over the last name. "Do you have to talk to her? I mean, you've got the Londell estate on paper."

"I don't know. If I can get any inside information about Jason or Juliana, it might help. I'm not sure what to ask her or if she'll give me any answers."

Her head bowed, she nodded.

"Em, you call Milner and see if we can get the document. I'll make inquiries and see who the Timmermeister lady is."

"Skip."

"What? You need more aspirin?"

She affected a weak smile. "Yeah, those too. No, I just feel conflicted."

Being hungover never left me feeling conflicted.

"Juliana and Kathy seriously want to see me amount to something as an actress. And here I am, trying to sabotage—"

"Em, I don't know how many ways I can say this." I was getting frustrated with her myopic view. "I'm like a CD with a bad scratch and it keeps repeating the same line of a song." What was it my mother used to say? Something about a broken record. "We're here because there's a good chance the lady, your agent, Juliana Londell, is accessory to a murder. That's the only reason we came to L.A. I'm conflicted too, okay? I know you want to give this gig a shot, but you should have picked a different agent because this one may be going to jail."

She bit her bottom lip and looked up at me as I pulled on my polo shirt.

"Well, I'll play it out as long as I can. And yes, I'll get the agreement between Jason and his wife. And by the way, I do have an appointment today. I forgot to tell you last night."

"What's that?"

"We're doing a table read this afternoon for the show."

"What's a table read?" The two of us were now speaking different languages.

"The actors in a specific episode read their lines with everyone else. It's the first run-through for the show. In this case, the pilot."

"You know, you're getting ready to actually do this thing, and I don't even know what the show is supposed to be about."

"What they've told me is, it involves a nerdy scientist who is working on developing cheap energy, and every time he comes up with something really great, it breaks down, burns up, falls apart, or something like that."

I thought about the concept for a couple of seconds. In some ways it sounded like the story of my life. Should have sold it to Hollywood.

"Doesn't sound funny to me."

"I know. I'm really anxious to do the table read this afternoon and see where the humor is."

"You're this guy's sister, right?"

"I am. From Detroit."

"Why Detroit?"

She shrugged her shoulders. "Gotta be from somewhere, Skip."

"But Detroit?"

She stood up, walked into the bathroom, and splashed cold water on her face.

"Okay, I've got calls to make, you've got calls to make."

"I'm on it."

Coming back to the bedroom, she finished her coffee and three aspirin tablets and seemed like she was getting herself back together.

"Em, you still haven't told me the name of this show."

"*The Edge of the Earth*," she said.

"Like, you might fall off?"

"Yeah. Just like that."

CHAPTER FORTY-ONE

I'd looked her up. The lady worked for an accounting firm in downtown L.A. There wasn't much information on the Timmermeister woman, but I called the number from my cell phone and was greeted by a friendly, young voice.

"McClain, Bryan, and Beldon," she said with a smile.

"Betsy Timmermeister, please."

"Can I tell her who's calling?"

"I wanted to talk to her about possibly doing my taxes."

The lady hesitated.

"Mrs. Timmermeister does some payroll taxes," the lady said, "is that what you're inquiring about?"

"Uh, sure. Payroll."

"She only works with a handful of selected clients. I don't believe she is taking on new business at the moment. I'm sorry. Now her main job with our firm is working with investment portfolios."

"So that's more than just accounting."

"Of course. She's more of an investment counselor. Did you have any other interest in our firm?"

"I'm more than interested in investment portfolios. That's a great place to start. Can I talk to her?"

The receptionist sounded relieved. I'd finally given her a reason to connect me with the Timmermeister woman.

"Let me see if I can reach her. Her schedule is somewhat complicated."

She put me on hold and there was soft, soothing music on the line, abruptly interrupted by a nasal female voice warning me that I should keep meticulous records of all my financial transactions. I didn't have that many. Then, back to the music. Finally, Betsy Timmermeister came to the phone.

"This is Betsy, how can I help you?"

"Your receptionist said you deal with investment portfolios?"

"I do. You see, I'm not a broker, but I work with brokers in a variety of fields. Real estate, business holdings, partnerships—"

"So you—"

"Make suggestions. Help people grow their portfolios."

I had no portfolio. I wasn't quite sure what one was.

"How much money would I have to have to approach you?"

"Where did you find my name?"

"A client of yours."

"Who would that be?" She sounded cautious.

"First of all, could you tell me how much I'd have to invest?"

"For me to accept you as a client, you'd have to have roughly three million dollars minimum that you could put at risk."

I couldn't speak. My chest was tight, and I was short of breath.

"Hello."

I believe I gasped.

"Okay," I uttered the word three times. "Okay, okay, three million."

"Yes. Do you have that much?"

If I counted the change in my pockets, I had at best four or five hundred dollars I might be able to lay my hands on. Who am

I kidding? I have maybe two hundred bucks if I sell my auto-graphed picture of LeBron James. And I'm not even sure if it's authentic. My business partner gave it to me as a birthday gift, and I'm never sure if what he says about things like a LeBron James autograph are the truth.

"Yes, I do."

And she'd said I had to have it to put at risk. At risk? If I had a couple thousand dollars, I certainly wouldn't put it at risk. It was crazy talk.

"Who recommended me?"

"He's no longer alive."

"Please, I'd like to know."

"Jason Londell. I worked with him in the last several weeks and he—"

"Jason Londell? Jesus Christ, who is this?"

A strange reaction to a referral. When someone recommend-ed me to install a security system, I was usually ecstatic. Maybe the fact that he was deceased unnerved her a little. I couldn't tell.

"Can we get together?" I just wanted an appointment.

"You worked with him how long ago?"

"In Miami. Just before he died."

"Oh, really?"

"Really." That part was the honest-to-God truth.

"What did he say about me?"

"Jason recommended you. I told him I'd come into some money, and he said if I wanted to invest, you were—"

"He actually told you to call me?"

"Yes. He said that you—" I hesitated. The Londell portfolio I saw looked like she had done a great job for the actor and his wife. I knew nothing about how it had grown or shrunk, but the sheer dollar amount told me I was in the presence of greatness.

I don't know what she thought he might say, but I was winging it. "He said that you did a good job, you had a variety of investments to choose from, and you were very thorough."

"He said that? Jason Londell? Two weeks ago?" I heard suspicion in her voice, and I wondered what she was thinking about me. Maybe I didn't sound as sincere as I should have. Or maybe she was surprised that Londell had praised her like I said he did. I started believing that I actually consulted him.

"Yes."

The lady was quiet for a moment, and I could hear her breathing on the other end. Some computer keys clacking, maybe a voice in the background, then she was back on the line.

"Why don't we plan on meeting tomorrow morning? Around ten?" she asked.

"That would be great." Or not.

"You have my address?"

"I do."

"All right, then. What is your name?"

I didn't want to give her any more information, but she kept pushing.

"I can introduce myself when we meet."

"That's not good enough. Sir, if we're going to meet tomorrow, I need your name. Right now."

"Yes, ma'am. Eugene Moore."

"Eugene?"

"Yes."

"M-O-O-R-E?"

"Yeah."

"Where are you from, Eugene?"

I said it before I thought. "Carol City, Florida, ma'am."

More clacks on her keyboard. Why would she possibly want to know that? I had three million dollars to invest. Wasn't that enough?

"Phone?"

If I wanted to bail, she was making it very difficult to.

"Phone." The tone was insistent.

I gave it to her.

"My assistant will call you half an hour before the meeting to make sure you are going to be here. And I will be in my office at ten a.m."

I knew where the office was located.

"I look forward to our meeting." I wasn't sure that I really did.

"It's an exploratory meeting. I'll be here, Eugene. Don't keep me waiting."

CHAPTER FORTY-TWO

I didn't know if it was legal to see a couple's prenuptial agreement or not, but I was certain it was illegal to copy a couple's investment portfolio, so I'd already broken one law. It was much easier going forward. Break one law, break two, ten, it made little difference at this point. If Gene Milner could produce the document, the infamous prenup, we would know exactly how Juliana had to perform. If she, Jason Londell's wife, didn't live up to the agreement, if she was proven unfaithful, that in itself didn't mean she'd killed Jason, but it certainly put a damper on her value. If she was proven unfaithful, she didn't inherit any of the investment portfolio. Life insurance, a different story.

Dropping Em off at Gene Milner's office, a hole-in-the-wall in a strip mall near East L.A., I waited outside. The area didn't look very safe with small groups of minorities walking the sidewalks, almost all of them checking me out. There were blacks, Hispanics, Asians, and strange-looking white dudes. One guy with a Mohawk haircut and tattoos covering his forearms spit on the car, and two dark-skinned women with handkerchiefs around their heads raised their middle fingers to me. I must have looked way too Anglo. I spent the time worrying about the insurance implications if someone would actually slam a hammer or bat into the vehicle, creating a dent that I couldn't pay for. It was a very dicey neighborhood.

Three-D graffiti was scrawled on the burrito carryout joint next door. *Juan's Burritos and Tacos.* Actually, the colorful graffiti was very artistic, peppered with what seemed to be Spanish words with 3-D effects and a brilliant burst of neon colors. Again, my art appreciation class at Samuel and Davidson University didn't really kick in, but I had no idea what good art was all about. I just knew what I liked. Bottom line was, I felt certain the graffiti carried gang overtones. L.A. was overrun with gangs. At least that's what we'd been told at the front desk of our cheap motel. The lady had, very quietly, offered to sell me a pistol. She said I'd probably need it. Now, I was questioning my reluctance.

Three male Latinos with blue-and-white bandanas strolled by my rental, eyeballing the Chevy and me. Then they walked back even closer. I closed my eyes as if taking a nap, praying they would see how cheap the car was and decide against a jacking.

When I opened my eyes, they had disappeared.

Em walked out five minutes later, a brown envelope in her hand. I breathed a sigh of relief. It was time to get the hell out of Dodge. Milner was behind her, a bear of a man with a ponytail and thick face, scowling as he watched her get into the rental car. I'd apparently interfered with his bad intentions.

"Got it, Skip. Jason Londell gave this prenup to Milner when he hired him to check up on Juliana."

"Does he have proof that she was unfaithful? Evidence? Maybe pictures or a recording?"

"He was very evasive. Said he'd taken photos, had some communications that he'd intercepted on her cell phone and computer, but he wouldn't share anything. He is working with Londell's attorney, some guy named Don Witter. I assume there's some sort of client confidentiality."

I didn't know. Hell, I was a private investigator with a license, but I had no idea if we were bound to keep all client information a secret. It wasn't like we were an attorney or doctor, where we'd gone to school for eight years and were sworn to uphold an oath. We were bottom-feeders. We took pictures of private moments, stole conversations and e-mail, copied people's files and, if we didn't get caught, if we got away with our deceitful and highly illegal and unethical tricks, we generally tried to make people's lives worse than they were. Maybe not all P.I.s, but James, Em, and me. And I'm sure Gene Milner was in that group. But, if Milner didn't want to share any more than he had, at least we had the prenup and that was a start.

"There was one thing that he said, then sort of backtracked."

"What?"

"He said, 'the inside scoop is.'"

"And then what?"

"He stopped."

"So he didn't want to explain?"

"I don't know, Skip. The inside scoop is—"

"That's it?"

"Could have been anything."

"Could have been he has some inside information."

"Anyway, I've got to be at the table read in half an hour. What are you going to do while I'm there?"

"I thought maybe I could sit through the read and see how it goes." I looked forward to being a part of the process. Maybe then I could start to buy into her obsession to be the next American princess.

"No. Skip, you were fired, remember?"

"I do remember that."

I couldn't forget.

"I think it's better if I go solo. I don't want these people thinking I can't take care of these things by myself. Pick me up in two hours and we'll debrief, okay?"

I dropped her off again, realizing I was somewhat like a chauffeur to a petulant new starlet. I'd had worse jobs. This one just didn't pay anything.

I stopped for coffee at a place called Ed's Coffee Shop on Robertson Boulevard. The place smelled like strong black coffee and frying sausage and had photos of some rather homely people on the wall along with some artwork by a guy named Michael Becker. I found out later the people in the photo were Ed and his wife from the sixties. The regulars who were scattered around the room were also on the unattractive side, but then I knew where all the beautiful people were at this moment. At a table read somewhere in La-La Land. Reading a script about a nerdy scientist and his sister from Detroit. I just wish I could have been there.

Over a cup of strong coffee with cream, I studied the paper Em had given me. The prenup was interesting to read. Just as the insurance policy kept repeating *however*, this document must have taken its lesson from the author of the ten-million-dollar insurance article.

This document will pay to the bearer, Juliana Londell, the full amount of blah blah blah, *however, in the case of an adulterous relationship*, blah blah blah. *The recipient will recieve* blah blah blah, *however, in the case of an adulterous relationship*, and it must have repeated that statement ten more times. If Juliana had a sexual affair with someone while she was in the boundaries of her marriage, *however* miserable that might have been, she did not qualify to receive seventy-five million dollars. She either slept with Jason or slept alone. It couldn't have been any clearer. For seventy-five million dollars? I think I'd keep it in my pants. But that's from a male perspective.

However, the ten-million-dollar insurance policy was not mentioned. I wasn't quite sure how she could live on a mere ten mil, but she got that regardless. *However*, my guess was that if she killed Jason, the insurance company would contest the payment. It was all above my pay grade and my understanding. How do you deal with financial complications of that magnitude when you make less than thirty thousand dollars a year? I could not fathom the amount of money involved.

I made .03 percent of what this guy, this Jason Londell was worth. Not even one-half of one percent. Three hundredths of one percent. I was trying to fathom that figure. The entire exercise seemed like a reason to introduce me to reality. Juliana Londell would be inheriting the entire fortune.

I was going nowhere fast, and there were people in my age range who were so far ahead that I could never dream of catching up.

CHAPTER FORTY-THREE

She was gushing, and I was getting used to it. The table read had been awesome. Yes, she actually used the word. Awesome.

Funny, oh, yes.

"There's a joke that they repeat a number of times, but it's the theme of the show, Skip. 'If anything *can* go wrong, it will go wrong just before your grant is up for review.'" She chuckled. "It works so well in the script."

A laugh a minute and the show could be, *should be,* a fabulous success. A cross between *The Big Bang Theory* and *Two and a Half Men.*

How could you fail with those two shows as your anchors?

"Skip, we were all laughing by the third minute. The writing is a hoot, and I really think I bonded with the guy who plays my brother. Well," she ran on and on, "I bonded with everyone there. The guy who plays the head scientist, Evan somebody, you've seen him on *How I Met Your Mother,* he came up to me after the read and couldn't say enough about how well I did. I just shrugged my shoulders and smiled. I mean, what do you say? I've never really acted before and then someone comes up to you and yadda yadda yadda yadda—"

I headed for the motel and a little peace and solitude. And, I wanted to call James. I needed to talk to him about the situation. Usually, to get some clarity, I call Em. She's almost always good for some straight talk. If I have some conflict, Em will straighten it out. Not this time.

We arrived an hour later and walked to our room without saying a word. She'd pretty much said everything she had to announce, and I'd kept quiet. It did me no good to rain on her parade.

I walked outside to call James just as he was calling me. Seven o'clock Miami time, so he must not have drawn a night shift.

"Skip, any more near-death experiences?"

"No, but I've got the prenup. And I've got the financial report. The guy was worth at least seventy-five million, James."

"What can you buy with seventy-five million, Skip? What?"

"Two vineyards in New Zealand, property on St. Barts, a row of townhouses in New York City, a waterfront penthouse in Florida, a publishing company—"

"Okay, okay, I get it. Maybe it won't be seventy-five million, but we're going to be worth some serious jack, amigo. Soon. Very soon."

"I'm just working on the case, James. No expectations. I've had some thoughts after talking to my girlfriend."

"I'm not sure where you're going, Skip, but I've got my own news. You may be able to shed some light on this."

"Yeah?"

"Don't know what it means, but it's interesting."

"Spill."

"Your buddy, Director Randy Roberts, and Mr. Clint Anders are flying back to California."

"James, you told me that the last time we talked."

"They left this morning, pally. Didn't mention it to anyone. They arrive the same time Londell's body arrives."

"A day early."

"Yeah. And they didn't tell Ashley. She's a little miffed. The three of them were supposed to be taking a private jet tomorrow, and those two took that private jet today. No explanation."

Private jet. I couldn't imagine what that might be like.

"What do you think happened?"

"No idea, dude. Ashley is going commercial tomorrow morning and production has shut down."

"So what are you doing?"

"Hey, the lady is springing for first class, pardner. And me, I'm with the blonde actress."

"Still sleeping with the client?" I didn't know whether to be pissed off or envious. But then I was sleeping with the up-and-coming Emily Minard, soon to be of some other name.

"Guilty," he said. "Still sleeping with the actress known as AA."

Things usually came up roses for my best friend.

"Speaking of sleeping with actresses, Em got the role, James. They had a table read today."

"Table read?"

"We have a different way of talking out here, Mr. Lessor. If you're coming west, learn to speak the language."

"Damn, Em on TV?"

"It appears."

"That just seems impossible."

"Don't tell her that. I think I remind her every hour."

"Anyway, maybe with the two of us we can get to the bottom of this murder."

"Two heads are better than—oh, one more thing, James. I've got an interview with a Betsy Timmermeister tomorrow morning at ten. She was Jason Londell's financial advisor, sort of. She seems to have managed his investments."

"Really? That's great news, dude. She's agreed to talk? About their financial situation?"

"Not exactly."

"So what's the interview?"

"I've supposedly got three million dollars to invest, and she's interested in managing it for me."

"You and your crazy girlfriend. You've been gone less than four days, and Emily is a movie star. You, you're now a multimillionaire. I can't wait to get out there, Skip. Imagine what *I'll* accomplish in three days. Off the charts."

"Wish me luck, James. I don't even know what I need to ask this Timmermeister lady, but I've been winging it ever since we got here and things keep falling into place. I feel certain that I'll figure it out."

"You don't have to show her the money tomorrow?"

"Exploratory meeting. That's what she called it."

"All right. Talk in vague generalities."

That wasn't going to be hard since there were no specifics.

"But," my friend continued, "turn the conversation to Jason. If he had that kind of money, who other than Juliana might have benefited from his death? Did this Betsy Timmermeister know Ashley Amber? Does she think Juliana might have had something to do with the death? If she'll visit that line of questioning then—"

"What possible reason do I give for questions about Londell? And to ask her if she thinks his wife killed him? Come on, James."

"Somebody killed him. Chances are there was some financial reason. She's the finance lady. Tonto, you are good at the question game. It will come to you."

"Yeah, maybe."

"We'll be in around two o'clock your time tomorrow, okay?"

"We'll pick you up at the airport."

"Skip, there'll be a limo waiting."

"Oh, yeah. You're with AA. Limos are a way of life, am I right? Where are you staying?"

"Way of life, Skip. Let me live that life for two or three days, okay? It ain't going to last forever. I know that. Where am I staying? That's a little tricky. She doesn't want her friends to jump on our minirelationship so she's staying at the Chateau Marmont, and I was wondering if you could arrange something at the place you're staying."

"What? She's embarrassed to be seen with you?"

He was quiet for a moment.

"Yeah. Something like that."

"So this is just a—"

"One-night stand? That's gone a little longer than one night? Pretty sure that's what it is."

"Too bad."

"Why is that, Skip?"

"Because, there's a chance you could be having a relationship with a lady whose sister is seriously rich. You know that game The Six Degrees of Kevin Bacon?"

He did. It was where everyone can tie into actor Kevin Bacon within six relationships. Usually fewer. You know a guy who knows a banker whose father lives in L.A. who plays golf at a country club where, well, you get the picture.

"Your new girlfriend may be one degree from being a multi-multimillionaire."

"Wouldn't that be nice?"

"Think about it, James."

"I hate to admit it, amigo, but I have."

And I knew damned well he had.

CHAPTER FORTY-FOUR

We had dinner at Nate'n Al Deli on Beverly Drive. I had a huge corned beef sandwich and Em had a salad. Now that she was in showbiz, she couldn't gain an ounce. These actresses.

No one hit on her, but customers were eyeing our table. She looks like she should be somebody and in this town, if you look like you should be somebody you probably are. At least a B actor. But, as I said, B actors are a dime a dozen.

"James and Ashley are coming in tomorrow. I got him a room at our motel. She's staying in the elite district."

"Glad you got him a room, because he's not sleeping on the sofa."

"Roberts and Anders are coming in tonight. A day ahead of schedule."

"Do you think there's any chance that they'll stop by the office? I'm supposed to be there tomorrow morning and go over some photos and stuff."

"It's going to be awkward if we run into them."

"Awkward? More than that. Randy Roberts doesn't know me," she said. "But Anders won't forget. How am I going to explain?"

"He might not recognize you."

"Trust me, Skip." She frowned and looked toward the ceiling. "I shouldn't tell you this, but Clint Anders gave me a lot of reasons to believe that he will remember our little talk."

Taking a deep breath, I exhaled loud enough for her to know I was annoyed. Tired. Exasperated. This was why she was so sure that Clint Anders was above being a suspect. Because he flirted with her?

"Does it get old having men hit on you?"

"You can't imagine. That's why I keep you around, to ward them off." She was being flippant. I was dead serious.

"So I'm like garlic around your neck? To keep the vampires away?" It wasn't meant to be a humorous comment.

"Exactly." She smiled and put her hand on mine across the table. "You're like garlic only you smell nicer."

I swallowed a spiteful comment, and we finished our wine and took a cab down to Kiss, a nightclub owned by Eva Longoria. Em had always liked *Desperate Housewives*, so we had a drink there. Then another and I had a couple more. I recognized a couple of TV people, one from *How I Met Your Mother*, but it wasn't like seeing De Niro or Demi Moore. I wondered if she was a distant relative. Demi Moore? I mean, she spelled her last name the same way.

We took an expense-tab cab back to our motel, like an old couple, not looking for a big party, realizing we both had things to do in the morning. In the back of my mind, I was worried about Clint Anders coming in early. According to James, he'd expressed a concern that I wasn't on the job, guarding and securing his precious TV set on a public park on Biscayne Bay. So now he was coming out here, his home territory. I made a firm decision to stay out of his way. I was definitely not going to the funeral, and I needed to keep looking over my shoulder. I remembered that L.A. and especially Hollywood was a small town.

CHAPTER FORTY-FIVE

We woke at six and even though I felt a little rough around the edges, we had some great morning sex before hauling ourselves out of bed at six thirty and showering. Breakfast started at seven thirty across the street at a diner, and I dropped Em off at her agent's office at nine. I prayed Anders was not going to visit Juliana today.

I was still a little groggy, having had about one too many drinks at Kiss the night before, but I had this sixth-sense buzz going on that everything wasn't exactly right, so I started checking the rearview mirror and, sure enough, a black BMW was hanging back, about four car lengths, making every turn with me and changing lanes every time I did.

I had time to kill before my ten o'clock, so I went on an expedition, trying to stay in tight proximity, but seriously having no idea of where I was. Turn left here, right there, drive one point two miles then turn around in a parking lot and head in the opposite direction. It was crazy.

I lost the car. Two minutes later, a black BMW was there. Three minutes later, it had disappeared. A minute later, there was a black BMW. And never close enough that I could check the license plate. Plus, I had noticed, there were a lot of black BMWs in town. Like Miami, pricey vehicles everywhere. In Carol City, an average car lot had cars starting at twenty-two hundred or less. In Miami, and Los Angeles, a cheap used car lot started pricing at twelve thousand dollars. And some much higher.

I'd lost sight of the BMW again and took a sharp right, almost rear-ending a Porsche. Two doors down was an alley, and I pulled in, parking the Chevy against the stucco wall of a building. I stepped out and walked back to the street. A black BMW had parked illegally just down the way, and it appeared the driver was still inside. Pulling my cap a little lower over my forehead, I slowly walked toward the car.

Just a walk by, turning my head to get a glimpse of who this person was. Guy, girl, someone who had tried to kill me?

Whoever it was may have realized I parked in the alley, but they couldn't have known it was me walking down the sidewalk. Just a local guy walking back to work or heading to the local poker palace or—

The passenger door swung open about two seconds before I approached the car, and I froze, looking to my right, my left, considering every direction except what was in front of me. The man stepped out, spun around, his right arm straight out, and I noticed the thick, black leather bracelet he wore. He kept on spinning, hitting me with a blow to the chest, and I doubled over, unable to breathe for several seconds. This guy must have had some serious training in the martial arts, because with just the arm and spin, he almost crushed my rib cage.

Bent over, temporarily out of breath, I realized I was the main target. Sometimes it takes me a while. Staying low, I sensed rather than saw the man relax as he walked closer and looked down at me. Taking two deep breaths, I thrust back up, jamming my head under his chin, and he gasped and fell backward onto the sidewalk, his skull making a solid thud on the concrete.

"Hey, man, no hard," I emphasized the word hard, "feelings."

I was dizzy for a second, the blow from my skull contacting his making me a little light-headed. Shaking my head, I tried to regain some sensibility.

"Hard feelings, asshole?" The voice was cold and threatening.

Shaking my head again, I turned to my left and there was the driver of the vehicle, a guy straight out of central casting. He wore a gray wifebeater tank top, tight jeans, what looked like Reebok canvas shoes, and he sported a goatee with his shaved black head. I also noticed that he was pointing a pistol at my temple.

The day had started so well, and now? Now I was so screwed.

CHAPTER FORTY-SIX

I can make a case that my brain was a little fried at the moment. Without being a doctor, I can guess that I had a mild concussion from the impact of my head on my attacker's skull. However, in my meek, mild-mannered lifestyle, I never thought I was capable of physically defending myself against the threat of a gun.

The gunman gestured that I should get into his BMW, and as I looked down and saw the guy with the leather bracelet struggling to get up from the sidewalk, it struck me that I'd just taken out the man who possibly murdered Jason Londell. The killer who assumed the name of cameraman Greg Handler. About thirty-five, short blond hair—

"Get into the car, asshole."

I'd taken down one man. I recognized the fact that the man I'd disabled was weaponless, but I was now empowered. If Em could be a princess, I could be a secret agent, a superhero, a spy, a killer.

Nodding at the gunman, I bent to get into the backseat. Again, I immediately sensed when he felt himself in control and relaxed. It was at that moment the adrenaline rushed in.

I leaned into the backseat of the plush vehicle and suddenly kicked back hard with my right foot. I landed a solid blow to the gunman's elbow, and the weapon spun out of his hand and landed with a skid ten feet away.

"You mother—"

He leaned in, attempting to drag me from the seat. I lashed out with my left foot this time, catching him on the chin. I heard a crack as he screamed. I couldn't believe it. Me, the guy who couldn't complete the rope climb in high school, the guy who got cut from the football team, here I was busting up bad guys.

Spinning around, I ran at full speed, back toward the alley, to the Chevy rental. Luckily I'd left it unlocked. I jumped in, slammed the door shut, and shot out of the alley back onto the main street. As I raced by the BMW, I saw the guy who played Greg Handler shouting into his cell phone. And his partner sprawled out on the street with the gun still on the ground. If they weren't trying to get me before, I was sure they would have plans to get me now.

And all of a sudden it hit me. Something I'd been trying to recall since the murder. The guy with the leather wrist strap, the guy who impersonated Greg Handler, had been given specific instructions to commit the murder. From Randy Roberts. I'd heard it and taken it as a camera direction. And maybe it was, but the direction from Roberts was about as direct as it could be. "Shoot this one." The line jumped out at me, and I could hear Roberts and see him mouth the words. He'd said, "Camera one, shoot this one. Okay, action." And five seconds later, Jason Londell lay dead on the ground, and camera one was nowhere to be found.

Of course, in that context *shoot* could be taken both ways. But Roberts had spoken directly to camera one, the cinematographer on the scaffolding. And he'd told him to shoot. Roberts was the last one to speak to Jason Londell and the last one to talk to camera one.

231

And Roberts was a former makeup artist, who with a little work, could transfer himself into the pudgy, big-nosed man we saw on the driver's license photo. The one who rented the camera.

It was a long shot, but it made sense to me. As I drove on, keeping my eye on the rearview mirror, I recalled the frantic phone call from Roberts. He wanted me to remember every second of what happened, because he needed a witness to corroborate his story. His story was that he was just directing. Just doing his job. And I assumed that's exactly what he was doing. Until now.

His directions to the camera guy, his background in makeup, and a grip who died of a drug overdose made me think that Randy Roberts was possibly a major player. And I wasn't sure why.

Calling James's cell phone, I got his voice mail.

"James, I just had a run-in with the guy who pretended to be Greg Handler. A gun was pulled, but I'm okay. I'll get back to you on that, but in the meantime check on Randy Roberts."

My roommate and his date may have been en route to L.A., but I figured he could look Roberts up when he landed.

"We should have done a background check on this guy. An alcoholic film guy who's bounced around doing a number of jobs, and the real Greg Handler says he's a pretty bad director. Greg Handler confronted him, telling him to lay off the booze. Now, why would Clint Anders hire someone like that? There have got to be some directors with real talent. You'd think. Anyway, if you get a chance, run a background search on him. We've known all along the guy was suspect. I'm headed to Betsy Timmermeister's office. Travel safe, dude."

"Camera one, shoot this one. Okay, action." I was going to suggest that it be engraved on Jason Londell's tombstone.

CHAPTER FORTY-SEVEN

Unless they'd attached a GPS to the car, I couldn't believe they would be able to follow me to Betsy Timmermeister's office.

About five blocks later, I slowed down to a reasonable speed. All I needed was to be arrested for speeding. My heart was still racing and I was sure my blood pressure was at the top of the chart. Taking several deep breaths, I tried to think calming thoughts.

McClain, Bryan, and Beldon was on the fifth floor of a modern, stone, twenty-story building, and the lobby of their floor was tastefully done with palm trees, a small waterfall, and a goldfish pond. I suppose with the volatility of the financial markets, this green space acted as a calming influence to frantic investors. As I was about to turn over three million dollars for investment, I drank in the beauty and serenity, took one more deep cleansing breath, and walked to the front desk.

"Betsy Timmermeister, please."

The receptionist, a leggy blonde with frosted highlights, walked me back through a row of offices. The Timmermeister lady's office was floor to ceiling windows and looked out on the Los Angeles skyline. A very impressive view.

She was standing, looking out those very same windows. She turned when I entered, and I saw she was an attractive brunette with cascading hair and a beautiful face. Not someone I would expect as an accountant or financial advisor. I'd expected the stereotype: glasses, no makeup, hair in a bun—

"Mr. Moore." She glanced at her cell phone face up on her desk. "Punctual, I see." There was no smile and no humor in her voice.

She continued standing, so I did too even though there were two comfortable armchairs a few feet away.

"Gaelic name, Moore."

I nodded, not sure where she was going with this.

"You have a father who left the family when you were young. A mother and sister, am I correct?"

I nodded again. If she knew even that much, she probably knew I didn't have a pot to piss in. No three million bucks. So now what was I going to do?

The lady continued to study me, hands clasped behind her back.

"What you may not know is, it appears there may be a Scottish robber baron in your background, not too many grandfathers ago. Maybe four. John More, spelled with one *o*. And without really doing all my homework, there's a chance that William Moore was also a relative. William being shipmates of the pirate Captain William Kidd. He was Kidd's gunner."

"You study genealogy."

"It's a hobby. I get to know a little bit about people this way."

"About our appointment."

"I'd like to take it out of the office if that's all right with you."

Picking up her purse from beside her desk and clutching her cell phone she motioned toward the door. We left by the back door of her office. The elevator let us out at a parking lot, and she motioned for me to follow her. I had no idea where we were going, and no idea how the conversation was going to end up. How long did I keep up the charade? And how should I respond to my dastardly past?

A robber baron and a pirate ship gunner. Not a savory group of relatives.

The lady pointed to a black Cadillac Escalade and got in on the driver's side. I hopped in and we took off.

"Do most financial interviews start out like this?"

"No. But I'll explain soon. I was impressed with your background and—"

"I didn't give you my background."

"True, but as you know, Mr. Moore, it's amazing what we can find on the World Wide Web. Am I right?"

She was. And this was not a good sign. James and I were on the web. With a cursory look you could find out we were in the investigation business. Still—

I didn't know enough about the city to know where she had taken me, but the area was definitely working class. Long warehouses dotted the landscape and there were front loaders, back loaders, and power shovels everywhere.

"This is where a lot of the studios store their props, their sets, their equipment, their costumes, this is the home of some of Hollywood's most valuable memorabilia." She swept her arm out to impress me with the vastness of the property. "These warehouses can be the birthplace for a brand-new movie or a graveyard for items that will never again see the light of day."

"And what does this have to do with our meeting?"

"There's a conference area in that building." She pointed to a steel-sided structure directly in front of her Escalade. "I'd prefer to talk there, if that's okay with you."

I put on a false bravado, but I was a little concerned that this lady had done more homework on me than I thought she would.

"Sure."

"Then let's go."

She got out and so did I. We walked across the cracked and pitted asphalt parking lot, me following at a two-step distance. I considered calling Em or James. There was this uneasy feeling that something wasn't quite right, and I wanted someone to be aware of the location of my body if all didn't go well. Of course, I may have been paranoid and maybe the lady was exactly who she claimed to be. But better safe than sorry.

I pulled my cell phone from my pocket, and she turned to say something.

"Put the phone away, Mr. Moore."

"Just calling my partner."

We had entered the building, and I noticed the dim lights highlighting a walkway through the center of the structure.

"Away, Mr. Moore. Put the phone away. I told you once. Please, don't ask me to tell you again."

I'd just laid out two thugs on the streets of L.A. I'd just proven that mellow guys can be bad asses too. Don't give me unreasonable demands. Just don't.

I looked into her eyes, ice-cold orbs, and nodded.

Shoving the phone back into my pocket, I followed meekly.

And I asked myself, what did I need a conference area for? There were two of us on an exploratory meeting. Two of us.

We walked down the hall, footsteps echoing off the steel walls. Reminiscent of *The Green Mile* or *Dead Man Walking*. Prison movies where someone was going to die.

"There's no reception in this building. The steel prevents any electronic signal." A warning.

I was tempted to check my phone again for bars, but a stern look from the financial guru warned against it.

Passing three unmarked doors on our left, we continued to the next, and she opened it and ushered me in. As promised, there was a small conference table and six chairs. A white board was mounted on an easel and a flat-screen TV monitor hung on the far wall. No windows, no wall hangings, just a stark, cold room with a polished concrete floor.

She motioned to a chair and I sat. Betsy Timmermeister continued to stand.

"We're waiting for someone," she said.

"Is this the way these meetings usually work?"

"Mr. Moore, how many financial advisors have you had for your three-million-dollars' worth of investments?"

"Several."

"I see." She kept an eye on the open door. "How much are you really worth?"

"Look, Mrs., Miss Timmermeister, I—"

"Jason Londell didn't recommend me, did he, Mr. Moore?"

The guy was dead. How could she know what he recommended?

"As I told you—"

"Jason Londell was in the process of firing me and the firm. We were about to lose one of the biggest accounts we had. You see, Mr. Londell wasn't at all happy with the way his financial interests were being handled. And he wasn't at all happy with me. So I know that there was absolutely no way he was recommending me or my company to you."

"And you're telling me because?"

"Because, as I told you, I'm somewhat impressed with your background, Mr. Moore."

"I'm afraid I don't understand. All you've told me about my background is that I may have come from some murderers and thieves."

"No, no, I'm referring to your more recent background. You've apparently gotten mixed up in some matters that are none of your concern, and it appears you've deliberately done so."

"How have I done that?"

"You and your girlfriend, Emily, you've misrepresented your-selves, and because of that, you've apparently caused a lot of trou-ble. You actually had some very important people in this town convinced you were the real deal. Very impressive. Although, as you may have surmised, this is a town of fools. A smart person can swindle just about anyone in Hollywood. Take actor Adam Sandler for instance."

Even before she mentioned Sandler's name, I had a bad, bad feeling about the direction this conversation was heading.

"Where did you get my name?" she asked. "No, don't tell me. You hacked Juliana's computer, we're pretty sure of that. Anymore, breaking into someone's computer files isn't so hard to do, is it? But in those files is pretty sensitive material. Obviously, not meant for your eyes."

"What makes you think I—"

"Hacked her files?"

I nodded.

"She keeps her camera on." She put on a smirky smile.

"Her camera?"

"On her monitor. The one people use for Skype? When you sat down at her desk to steal the files, you were looking straight into the camera on her computer monitor, Mr. Moore."

She again smiled at me. The dumbest guy in the world. The stupidest man on the planet. Checking all the cameras in the neighborhood, on the buildings, in the doorways, outside and inside a bar, and even a traffic camera. And I'd missed the most obvious camera of all. Right in front of my damned face.

Pushing the chair back, I stood up.

"Obviously, this meeting wasn't for financial advice, and I apologize for that. Please forgive me."

"What did you expect? Seriously. What did you think was going to happen? That I didn't do homework on you? From the moment we met, you knew I had you figured out. Didn't you? What did you think you were going to get out of this meeting?"

"Information, I guess. I'm not sure. Information on Jason and Juliana's arrangement. You probably know that I'm working for a client who thinks that someone in Hollywood might have been responsible for Jason's death, and I was hoping to get information from you. Since you obviously know now that I'm not client material, I'll—"

"You'll what," she barked. "You'll just leave quietly? You stole valuable information from a client of mine and—"

"I thought you said they fired you."

"Two things wrong with that statement. I never said *they*. I said Jason. And, I never said he *fired* me. I said he was going to. You're a thief, Eugene. We've got the evidence. So I think you'd be smart to sit down and wait until my friend arrives."

Damn cameras. They are everywhere.

I heard footsteps echoing down the hall and gripped the arms of the chair. God knows who her friend was, but I was not anxious to find out. All I know is I never should have listened to James when he told me to break into the Londell/Bavely office. "It's a misdemeanor, Skip. No problem."

She walked into the hall, and I could hear a faint conversation. Grabbing my phone, I pushed speed dial for James. Without hanging up, I slid the phone back in my pocket. My luck he was on a plane and had his cell phone turned off.

A moment later she walked back in, Randy Roberts two steps behind her.

CHAPTER FORTY-EIGHT

"Security team sends their best. They miss you."

I stood up, hand out to shake his, but he didn't seem interested.

"Sit down, Moore."

"No, I think it's time for me to leave."

"Not yet."

As if on cue, he reached behind himself with his right hand and pulled out a pistol. I'd faced down one armed man today already, and I'd done pretty well. Now I was pressing my luck.

Glancing at Betsy Timmermeister, he said, "Teller called. Apparently our boy wonder here did some serious damage to Mitch."

I could only guess that Teller was the camera guy who impersonated Greg Handler and Mitch must be the driver with the broken jaw.

Buoyed up by today's experiences, I addressed him. "Tell me, Randy, it took me forever to figure out, but it was you who dressed up in that ridiculous garb and rented the camera, right? As Greg Handler?"

His stoic look was almost an acting pose. A humorous look and I had to stop and think that these people could kill me without blinking an eye.

"Come on, man, it was a bad makeup job. You knew it going in, right, Randy?"

No response. And surprisingly, I was calm. I just didn't see him killing me here in this isolated room with a professional financial advisor as witness. Then what better place? Maybe I should have been a little more concerned.

"Look, I can make guesses all day long, but seriously, why am I here? Why? I don't have any proof of anything. I'm just trying to make some money on the side. Get a couple bucks from my client. That's all."

"You broke into an office, you stole important documents. You think that actions don't have consequences?"

"So what are you going to do with me? Turn me into the LAPD? Then do it. Come on."

"Who is your client?" Betsy Timmermeister walked up to me, a cruel gleam in her eye.

"I can't say."

"Mr. Moore, Mr. Roberts has a gun. He wants to know who your client is. If you don't tell him, I may ask him to use the weapon."

I just couldn't buy into the cold-blooded killer routine from the Timmermeister lady. Roberts, yes.

"Bavely? Kathy Bavely?"

I took a step back. I was sure everyone knew. Certain. There could be no doubt that Ashley Amber was my client. And why would Bavely have hired me? Maybe because they knew Bavely had been keeping tabs on all of Juliana's meetings and boyfriends. And they thought hiring a private investigation company would give her help and advice. To be honest, I wasn't sure why Kathy Bavely was keeping tabs on her. Did she have a personal vendetta against Juliana Londell?

241

"Look," Roberts sat down, motioning to me to do the same. With a gun aimed squarely at my chest, I thought it was a good idea to follow suit.

"We know that Kathy Bavely has been trying to break the Londells up for some time. She's been caught on Juliana Londell's Skype camera several times. She doesn't know we caught her, but we did."

And I was even trying to figure out why Randy Roberts was involved. It didn't seem to make any sense. But if he'd been involved with the murder of Jason Londell, then he was trying to cover his ass.

"We know you were hired by Bavely," he said. "Kathy Bavely suspected that Juliana Londell had been unfaithful to Jason, but she couldn't prove it. And because she thought that Juliana might have been behind the murder of her husband—"

He kept swinging the pistol, waving it back and forth, and for just a split second, I considered rushing him. Probably not a good idea.

"How much is Kathy paying you? Enough that you would risk jail time for breaking into the office and stealing records?"

I didn't know if I was being set up or what. The entire situation was ludicrous. How could Randy Roberts and company not know that Ashley Amber was the one who was paying us?

And, again, the mind is an amazing tool. Like a computer, it comes up with answers you never even asked. They thought Kathy Bavely had hired us. And that triggered my venture through Bavely's computer. The one thing I hadn't figured out. Over and over Bavely had written on the calendar, ph A A. A A. Ashley Amber. Ph. Phone? Was she in touch with Amber? Were they communicating? Was there a conspiracy to prove that Juliana Londell was cheating on Jason? Ph A A. Phone Ashley Amber. Or did it mean that Juliana was calling her sister? Sometimes twice a day. Ph A A. It had to be phone Ashley

Amber. I just wasn't sure who was calling her. And even if I was right, it didn't appear that was going to do me much good now.

"Jason Londell was shot." I held his gaze. "And, as surprised as you appeared, Randy, you directed the entire episode. I'm right, aren't I? It was probably the best episode you ever shot in your career. You should have gone into acting. You were very convincing, dude."

There was no way I was going to talk my way out of this. No way I could plead innocence. No way they'd let me walk out the door. I knew it, they knew it. So it seemed to me the best thing to do was keep delaying the inevitable. Keep talking. Keep ad libbing. Don't let them get to the next step, because I was afraid I knew what the next step was. Killing me.

"Kid, you messed with the wrong people."

"I'm not really sure who the people are, but let me guess."

"There are no guessing games," the Timmermeister lady stood and walked toward the door. "It's time we left."

"No, humor me." I raised my voice to her, tired of other people calling the shots.

"Randy, you directed the shoot. I watched you, and I had no idea what you were staging. I bought into your little act. And, just like you probably got actress Audrey Love to overdose on prescription medication, you found a way to kill the grip Andy Hall with the same method. A simple overdose. Why? Hall came to you and told you he suspected you were involved in Londell's murder? That must have been it. Protecting your story, am I right?"

Pausing and catching my breath, I kept on going. "You killed Hall. I assume he was a threat. Is it true that once you kill, it just gets easier every time you do it?"

He smirked, shaking his head.

"You should have been a screenwriter, Moore. Great imagination."

And again on the calendar that Kathy Bavely had put together for Juliana when I hacked her computer, I remembered the meetings with C.A. and B.T. Over and over. C.A., Clint Anders, and B.T., Betsy Timmermeister.

"And Miss Timmermeister, you were financial advisor for not only Jason Londell, but Clint Anders too."

She didn't deny it.

"Do you understand, Mr. Moore, you've committed a felony, stealing personal financial information?"

I spread my hands wide open on the conference table. "At this point, does that really make any difference? You are all involved in a murder. A murder, for God's sake. Maybe several. That makes copying personal financial information seem pretty petty, doesn't it?"

"I think this has gone far enough," she said. Opening the door, she pointed at me, but I stayed glued to my seat. The minute I stood up, I was afraid my fate was sealed. They'd be in charge and could kill me any time they wanted. I didn't move.

"You are the financial advisor for Jason Londell and for Clint Anders. Am I right, Miss Timmermeister?"

Her sharp glance to Roberts told me I'd scored a point.

"You, Anders, and Juliana are pretty tight, aren't you? You get together for lunch, have meetings together."

"How would you know that?" Her voice reverberated in the small room.

"Time to go," Roberts said.

"Anders is having trouble with his production company." I didn't move. "He's behind on some payments, trying to cut costs, cutting back on filming, among other things. Maybe he's, I don't know, gambling a lot?"

I saw a glimmer in Roberts's eyes. He knew that Anders had some indulgences.

"Paying for expensive hookers?"

"Jesus, stop. Get him the hell out of here, Roberts." Betsy Timmermeister was practically screaming at Randy, and I was afraid my time of bluffing might be coming to an end.

"Just tell me. Please. Was this a way to get Londell's fortune?" There was no other reason.

"Close to eighty million in assets, a ten-million-dollar insurance policy to Juliana, and what? Six or seven million dollars to Anders if the show was disrupted?"

"Now." Roberts walked up, grabbed me by the sleeve of my T-shirt, and yanked me to my feet, his gun pointing directly at my face.

"Come on, Randy. Almost one hundred million dollars. How much were you going to get? Being the guy who had to actually kill people. Well, you and, what was his name? Teller?"

And it all came together. It was a scheme to split the Londell fortune plus all the insurance money they could get.

"Yeah. That's what it was." Roberts pushed me into the hallway. "That's exactly what it was. You know, Moore, when there's a pool of money that big, there's enough to go around. No greed. And believe me, there's more than enough to go around. One guy gets out of debt—"

"Shut up." Betsy Timmermeister shouted at him, but he ignored her.

"Someone gets out of a bad relationship and is compensated for her suffering."

"Honest to God, Randy, you don't need to—"

"One lady," Roberts said, pointing at her, "gets the fruits of her labor, and one of us doesn't have to worry about climbing up the ladder in this industry. Ever again. Instead of begging for recognition, pleading for jobs, all his problems go away. He has more than he can possibly use. Not that that's a bad thing." Roberts smiled as he shoved his gun barrel into my back.

"Teller?" I asked.

"Teller? I can't see much of a cut at this point. He couldn't even deal with you. There's the punch line, Moore. Our shooter couldn't even deal with a low-level punk like you. That's the funniest story out there. I'm trying to figure out who they should cast as Teller when they make the movie. Curly, Moe, or Shemp?"

CHAPTER FORTY-NINE

He didn't pull the trigger. Instead, we all got into the Escalade. Timmermeister drove. There was no more conversation. About fifteen minutes into the drive, I started to recognize the neighborhood. I'd walked it, scouted it, and burglarized it. We were on the same street where Londell's office was located.

Parking across the street, Roberts ordered, "Out." He encouraged me with a push of his handgun.

I stepped down and crossed at the light, walking toward the office building. I thought about the cameras. The stoplight camera, the two cameras mounted in the doorway, the cameras mounted to the outside wall less than a block away. They were all monitoring our miniparade, and could be used, I suppose, as evidence in the case surrounding my murder. I didn't see that they had any other choice.

And as I wondered about my murder, I thought about Em. Now that they knew, her dream of acting had probably come to an end. And there would almost certainly be a second murder. And yet it all seemed surreal. Everything so far was phony. The fact that James, Em, and I were being paid to *investigate* a murder when we were often clueless, the phony résumé and union card, a phony cameraman, so maybe my imminent death was phony as well. I was a lot calmer than I thought I'd be under the circumstances. I actually was more worried about Em. She'd almost pulled off a modern-day miracle, and no one would ever know.

Roberts pushed open the door, and we entered Londell and Bavely's domain.

The Waronker lady was not at her station, and Kathy Bavely's office door was open with no sign of the agent.

Juliana Londell and Em sat in Juliana's office, talking across the desk.

"Ah, there you are, Randy. Betsy." She stood up and strode out to the lobby. "Mr. Moore, the boyfriend and fired agent." A bright smile was on her face, the first real toothy smile I'd seen.

"You had me going, Mr. Moore. You really did. You were good. I thought you two were the real thing. But then, I think Kathy brought some credibility to the situation. I didn't realize at that time that she was involved with you. Exactly when did she hire you and Emily?"

Again with the Bavely-as-client theory. I didn't say a word, but glanced back to the office and saw Em watching us.

"Oh, your girlfriend? She doesn't understand just yet that we know. Do you want to tell her, or should I?"

I said nothing.

"Emily, come out here."

Em approached cautiously. I wanted to just tell her to run for it, but she would have hesitated, slightly confused, and anyway Roberts had a gun. A gun almost always dictates the call.

"I must admit, Emily, I'm very disappointed. I really thought you had something. I mean that. I seriously expected you to go somewhere. Possibly my finest hour in the industry. Someone off the street who makes it big-time. But, I've learned that life isn't always what you expect it to be."

Em's eyes were wide open. She'd seen the pistol by Roberts's side.

"This is Betsy Timmermeister."

Juliana motioned to the Timmermeister lady.

"Betsy is my financial advisor. She helped Jason accumulate quite a portfolio of investments, as you know. Your ex-manager discovered just how much on the computer when he broke into my office."

"Juliana, what is this? What do you think—"

"You're not *that* good an actress, Emily. You got me, okay. But now that we have all the evidence, I realize I should have figured this out one hundred times by now. I wanted to believe I could pull this off."

I thought Em was a great actress. She'd almost become a two-day wonder, a star on her first attempt. And if it all ended here, she'd accomplished more than ninety-nine and nine-tenths of actors in this town ever did.

"Kathy Bavely is running an errand for me, Mr. Moore. Once we have taken care of the two of you, she will meet with an unfortunate accident and—"

"Bavely isn't involved." I had to keep this going. The end was much too near.

"Oh, we know that—"

"Your sister hired us. Neither of us had ever heard of Kathy Bavely until we arrived in L.A."

"Ashley?"

"Ashley. Do you have other sisters?"

I was pretty sure she didn't.

"The two-time widow? She hired you? No kidding."

Juliana genuinely sounded surprised.

"It makes no difference. Kathy's involved, trust me."

Roberts opened the office door, escorting us out onto the sidewalk. I don't know why one of us didn't run, except that the other would have been left behind.

"Where are we taking them?" Juliana stared at the Escalade across the street.

"Warehouse number three." We walked back across the street. "There's no reason Betsy has to go," Roberts said.

"We've worked too hard to get here," the Timmermeister lady said. "I want to be there to see that all the loose ends are tied up."

So our parade continued and we all got into the Escalade, Juliana sliding behind the wheel. I wondered what happened to rental cars when they're not returned. Maybe they have GPS units installed so they can track them down. They'd find mine down by Bavely's office with half a burger inside an In-N-Out Burger sack on the floor of the backseat. A sad souvenir of our trip to the movie capital of the world.

Juliana pulled away from the curb, and as I glanced out the window, I saw a black BMW cruising in the left lane beside us. The windows were tinted so I couldn't see inside, but it wouldn't be a surprise to see Mitch and Teller giving us an escort. I had a feeling that both of those guys would love to get their hands on me.

"I've seen your prenup, Mrs. Londell. Pretty specific about fooling around on your husband."

She turned her head for a brief instant and looked at me in the backseat.

"You've been a busy boy, Mr. Moore."

"I've seen you in a lip-lock with Rob Mason, but that was after Jason died. There was somebody before that wasn't there?"

Em was sitting next to me, shaking her head, as if to tell me to shut up.

She was silent.

"Juliana, it was Clint Anders wasn't it?"

All those meetings with C.A. It had to be.

"Who caught you?"

Em nudged me, hard. I didn't see why I should stop now. Whatever I said or didn't say wasn't going to change the outcome of our trip.

"Did Jason walk in on you?"

"Shut the fuck up, Moore." Roberts pointed the pistol directly at my forehead. He wasn't stupid enough to fire a gun in the middle of Los Angeles traffic. I didn't think.

"No, it wasn't him. I saw on the calendar he was on location in Singapore for that month."

She looked over her shoulder one more time.

All of a sudden I realized that Greg Handler was right. The mind is an amazing thing. It can put pieces of the puzzle together while you're not even trying. Jason Londell was on location while Juliana Londell was seeing Clint Anders.

"You and Anders, you set up the Miami shoot. Oh, my God, you had to kill Jason to keep him from finding out."

"Finding out what?" Em asked, looking at me as if I'd lost my mind.

"Em, Jason Londell wasn't even in the country when the kid was conceived. That baby bump you said she was hiding with her serape, it belongs to Juliana Londell and Clint Anders."

That's when I heard the clash of metal on metal, and we were thrown out of our seats.

CHAPTER FIFTY

The Escalade careened to the right, and Betsy Timmermeister banged her head on the rear passenger door glass with a thud. Em and I followed her, sliding across the leather seat.

Juliana straightened up, keeping control of the vehicle, and I noticed Roberts's face, grim as he gritted his teeth. He steadied the gun, pointing into the back seat.

"What the hell was—"

A jolt and the grinding of metal on metal as we were hit again. This time we held on a little tighter. I glanced out the window to my left as the BMW pulled away.

Juliana gripped the steering wheel, her knuckles white. As she slammed on the brakes, the BMW took one more hard swerve into our Cadillac, the car teetering as we crashed into the curb. This time I was ready.

Throwing myself over the passenger seat, I grabbed for the gun in Randy Roberts's right hand. Surprised, the man jerked away, his trigger finger pulling back as the pistol exploded, the bullet plowing through the firewall into the engine compartment. Sparks flew from where we caught the concrete curb, and the car went up and onto the sidewalk, grinding to a stop with the front end hung up on a street sign that said "No Loitering." I grabbed the gun, gave a good hard pull, and yanked it from his hand. Em was upright, watching all the action as I lowered myself into the backseat.

"You took a concealed weapon class?"

She nodded her head.

"Here." I handed her the gun.

As I started to open the door, Roberts reached back in desperation. As he grabbed for the pistol, Em showed him she knew how to use it. Grabbing it by the barrel, she swung the handle down, hitting his temple and clipping his right ear, leaving a gash where blood flowed freely. He fell back into the front passenger seat as my side door was pulled open.

James Lessor stood there smiling.

"Come on, pard. You, Em, it's time we got the hell out of here."

"Your car still running?"

"We're going to find out."

James climbed into the passenger side of the BMW, and Em and I scrambled into the back as I heard sirens in the distance. Ashley Amber turned from the driver's seat.

"We need to hang out more. You guys are a lot of fun."

"Where did you learn to drive like that?" Em asked.

"I took a course in stunt work. Pretty thorough actually."

When she stepped on the gas pedal, the beat-up BMW took off, and I turned to watch steam rising from the engine of the Cadillac.

Em leaned in and whispered softly in my ear.

"What I said about her? I take it all back. Every word."

CHAPTER FIFTY-ONE

We did what any law-abiding citizens would do. We found a cop and gave him an abbreviated version of what had happened. Two days later and after several hours of interviews, the worst part seemed to be over. When we met with the cops, they separated us and grilled each of us over and over again in these tiny investigation rooms like you see on TV shows. One table, three chairs, and station-house coffee. Apparently, our stories matched, because they finally let us go.

This was the first time we'd had a chance to really talk to each other since Em and I had left Miami.

"Battery on the phone gave out a while before we found you, amigo, but by then I knew you were headed to the office, and we knew who was with you."

"Betsy Timmermeister told me there was no signal in the steel building, but I decided I had nothing to lose by trying. So I called you."

We were in Ashley Amber's suite at the Chateau Marmont, and I decided I could get used to this kind of living. Room service had brought drinks, shrimp and cold lobster hors d'oeuvres, and fresh strawberries courtesy of Ashley Amber, and we were sipping pink champagne on ice. *Hotel California* stuff. The song had actually been written about this place.

"When I answered your call, we'd been on the ground for just a short while. I thought you must have butt-dialed me because the voices were muffled."

"Phone was in my pocket, James. She'd forgotten about it, and I was praying you would pick up and realize I was in a jam. Thank God, you kept listening and didn't hang up."

"Ashley had a limo lined up, but when we realized you were going to Londell/Bavely, we decided to rent a car and give you a little protection."

"Some rental company isn't going to be happy."

I pictured the BMW, banged in a million places, dented so much you wouldn't even recognize the brand.

"That's what insurance is for, Skip." She actually knew my name. Of course, she'd been sleeping with James, so it was nice she got it right.

"We heard enough to understand they were planning on killing you. Couldn't let that happen."

"Thank God," Em said.

"You knew your sister was sleeping with Clint Anders, right?" I wanted to make sure I had the information correct.

"No. I knew she was pregnant, and when I did the math, there was no way that Jason could have been the father. He was gone almost forty days in Singapore for that movie shoot." She paused. "And, I was aware of the prenup. If Jason Londell could prove Juliana was unfaithful, she got nothing. She was really pissed about that."

James reclined in an easy chair, sipping his second champagne. It would be only a matter of time before he switched to beer.

"Amber also knew that Clint Anders was running low on funds," he said. "She watched the cutbacks on the show, slow down on the mixes, and there were weeks when paychecks were late. Really late. Right, babe?"

He looked at her to continue the narrative.

"Plus, Clint was gambling a lot and losing," she said. "And FX and ABC had cut two shows he was producing. There just wasn't that much income. I guess Anders knew that Jason was going to figure out eventually that the baby was Clint's. And knowing he could get a pretty decent payout on Londell's insurance policy if Jason was killed, invited Londell to Miami to be on his show."

"Wow," Em was genuinely amazed, "Londell must have really liked Clint Anders to do the guest shot for him. A big-time movie guy doing a low-rated television show."

"Oh, he did like him," James said. "He thought he and Anders were best of friends, but since Jason Londell and his wife were separated—once he found out she was pregnant—Jason decided to do a little interaction with Amber, too. Right, babe?"

I swear the blonde blushed.

"So, he started a relationship with you?" I was intrigued.

"We'd always flirted, even when he was married to my sister," she said. "And after he found out she was pregnant by another person, he needed someone to talk to. He couldn't believe Juliana had cheated on him. We'd spend hours on the phone, then the chance to see each other came up when Clint invited him to Miami."

"You had no way of knowing Clint Anders wanted to kill him."

"No. How could I?"

"It is diabolical what those two planned," Em said.

"Oh, yeah." Ashley nodded in total agreement. "A seven-million-dollar life insurance policy made out to CA Productions.

And as long as no one could prove Clint and Juliana were having an affair—"

"And a baby," James said.

"There was the entire investment portfolio, which Juliana apparently offered to share with Anders if he'd keep things quiet."

"Not to mention a ten-million-dollar policy that Londell had given his wife."

"About one hundred million dollars if Jason was killed."

"Enter Randy Roberts," I said.

"Yeah, I'd worked with him," Ashley grimaced. "Not a nice man and a really bad director. I figured that Clint hired him because he was cheap. No one wanted the guy. He was drunk most of the time and could be an abusive asshole to the cast."

"But, he'd had some experience."

"Experience in killing someone. Audrey Love. She was an actress who got a little out of hand with her attitude and work ethic, and Roberts was asked to intercede. The producer had taken out a life insurance policy on her and thought maybe he'd like to cash in on it."

"To be fair," James said, "there's no proof. It seems pretty clear Roberts killed her with an overdose, but it was never proven."

"Unbelievable." I was having a hard time comprehending the whole thing.

"Clint Anders knew a little about the situation, since he was the producer on that show, so when he decided to take out Jason Londell during *Deadline Miami*, he called his buddy Randy Roberts. Roberts contacted Oscar Teller who had whacked a couple of drug guys here in L.A. and together they concocted this crazy scenario that actually played out better than most of the plots on *Deadline Miami*." Ashley finished her champagne and tilted the bottle to pour some more. She was getting a little tipsy.

"And," I continued, "Randy Roberts puts on a disguise, assumes a new name, forges identification, and rents the camera. He picked the name Greg Handler because Handler had accused him of being a drunk and a really bad director several years ago. Seemed like a way to pay Handler back."

"Why didn't the shooter, Oscar Teller, just rent the camera? He was playing cameraman, so it would have made sense." Em had a point.

"Think about it, Emily." Ashley took another sip of the potent pink bubbly wine. "Oscar Teller knew nothing about cameras. He was going to shoot Jason Londell, so he knew handguns, but he would have been lost if the clerk at Howell had started to talk technical with him. Randy Roberts knows cameras and he was the natural one to rent the unit. With a heavy disguise."

"And," I pointed out, "a company credit card."

There was silence as we sat around the room, each recalling some of the nightmare we'd all been a part of.

"Have they got Teller?" I wanted to know what happened to the fake who pulled the trigger starting this entire mess.

"Got him at a local hospital. His friend Mitch admitted him when he wouldn't wake up. Who knows if they'll be able to prove he pulled the trigger."

Would Teller simply walk? I hoped not. The guy had tried to kill me, twice.

"Betsy Timmermeister, how did she become a part of this?"

"Good question," James said. "My understanding is that Juliana Londell started making appointments with her, telling her that Jason was thinking about firing her. She told Betsy if she wanted her commissions to continue, and they were sizable, that she should work with her."

"I don't know if my sister told Betsy that the plot involved killing Jason," Ashley said, "but she convinced Betsy that Jason was going to dump her and turn the portfolio over to someone else. And Betsy didn't want to take the chance of losing that revenue."

"Juliana Londell. What a devious bitch," Em said.

"And Kathy Bavely?" I asked.

"Oh, she was the genuine thing." Ashley nodded enthusiastically. "Wanted a shot at becoming a real agent. When Juliana hired her, she couldn't believe her good luck. I think she saw through Juliana almost from the beginning, and she started keeping a record of whom she met with and what she was doing." She gave me a sidelong glance. "Well, you found out about that, Skip. Anyway, one thing led to another and Bavely even got in touch with Gene Milner, Jason's detective. She was feeding him some good information, but I think Milner was a skirt chaser and spent more time and Jason's money hustling women and running up charges at Chateau Marmont."

"Kathy says she's going to keep the agency open. Wants to still represent me, even after our little deception," Em said.

I shook my head.

"I didn't say I was going to go along."

"So what happens to the cast?" I asked. Ashley seemed to have most of the answers.

"I think Betsy Timmermeister walks." She shrugged her bare shoulders, her blouse pulled down over the ivory skin. "Juliana and Roberts will try to implicate her, but she pleads ignorance. She didn't know what was going down. The poor woman was just trying to service her customer."

"I don't believe it."

"Skip, here's something else you won't believe. I think Clint Anders may walk as well."

"What?" Em almost screamed.

"He was hands off. Randy Roberts will point all kinds of fingers, but Anders was never there. He wasn't on set when the murder occurred, and he wasn't a part of the kidnapping of you and Em, and nobody except Roberts has any evidence that he was involved. As far as anyone can tell, he told the truth. He turned the hiring of the camera guy over to Randy Roberts, and someone stole the company credit card."

"But he is the father of Juliana Londell's baby?" Em was trying to make the case.

"I'm sure there will be tests, but it's a safe bet. Doesn't make him a killer."

"Oscar Teller, the fake camera guy?" I asked. "He could implicate Anders, couldn't he?"

"Only reported to Roberts."

I couldn't believe it. Two of the four might walk away and start the next plot.

"The grip that overdosed?"

James gave me a sad smile. "There are always casualties that can't be explained, Skip."

"Okay," Em said, draining her second glass, standing up, walking to the window, and looking out on Sunset Boulevard, "why would a lady with let's say seventy-five to eighty million dollars at risk, not have an abortion? She's willing to kill her husband, but when it comes to killing the unborn child in her womb—"

Ashley nodded. "Flesh of my flesh, blood of my blood," she said.

"From a movie you did? A play?"

She smiled, brushing her blonde hair from her classic face. "Genesis 2:23."

"Ah." The lady surprised me more and more.

"And a rap song from DMX. Really good shit," she said.

"Oh."

CHAPTER FIFTY-TWO

James had flown back. Amber stayed. *Deadline Miami* was in limbo and the network was reportedly ready to cancel. All the hype and publicity in the world can't save a really bad product and apparently this was a bad product.

He'd stayed for the funeral and what an event. Hundreds of people convened at The Liberty Chapel at Forest Lawn. There were film clips, long speeches by Tom Hanks, Tom Cruise, writer Michael Connelly, and a host of other Hollywood celebs. Ashley Amber closed the ceremony, telling the assembled that Jason Londell was as peaceful as a quiet river. I had no idea what that meant. She spoke to his gentle nature and professed a love and respect that had come late in their relationship. I was pretty sure the relationship had lasted several weeks, but I could be wrong.

"Have you heard the latest, Skip?"

He was on the phone from Miami, back to cooking on the line at Cap'n Crab in Carol City.

"There's a lot of latest, James. They're still sorting out the cast of characters."

"I talked to Ashley."

"Yeah? I assumed she was moving on."

"Oh, I don't have any illusions," he said.

"Good thing."

"Guess who wrote out a new will?"

"I have no idea."

"Lawyers are going over it with a fine-tooth comb, but it appears that Jason Londell wrote an amendment to his will. If Juliana did not qualify to meet the criteria of the prenup—"

"Oh, no. No. No. No. No. Positively no."

"Yep. Ashley Amber gets half of the estate. The other half goes to some charity to benefit actors who are down on their luck."

"Fifty million dollars?"

"Something close to that."

I tossed and turned that night and couldn't hold a thought in my head. The fairness of life escaped me, except the part where there was no fairness. I drifted between the kidnapping sequence and the car wreck to the death leap. As soon as my mind had wrapped itself around one scene, another took its place. The look inside the Howell store with all the movie gear, the night where I met the sultry star of *Deadline Miami* in my trailer and I was dressed only in boxer shorts. I focused on Em and me at the Hollywood eatery where Dwayne Johnson came on to her, and just as I drifted off to sleep, Em's cell phone rang. Glancing at my cell, I saw it was nine a.m. Noon in Miami.

I heard her sleepy voice as I lay there, my eyes still closed.

"What? You've got to be kidding."

She was quiet for a minute, then, "Oh, my God. I thought there was no question."

Another long pause.

"Okay. I'll get back to you. Tomorrow? Let me think about it."

She turned, pulling her pillow tight under her head.

"You got your wish, Skip."

I had no idea what my wish was at this point.

"They canceled the show. The sitcom. Before it ever filmed the first episode."

"Because of the Juliana story?"

"No. Kathy said nothing is for sure, even when an episode is in the can. There are hundreds of reasons."

The Edge of the Earth would never see the light of day. I was surprised at my reaction. I was seriously disappointed even though it's what I'd wished for until it happened.

"You know," she said, "it really wasn't that funny."

We had coffee outside at a small bistro.

"She wants me to stay. Thinks I can nail another part. In fact, there's a reading tomorrow."

"What do you want?"

"I'm going to call Dad. If he can get a temp to cover some things, I can do some of his work from here."

"So?"

"Get a flight back, Skip. I'm going in for the read and maybe hang around for a couple of weeks. I think Kathy has a real interest in my career."

I nodded. It took twenty minutes to clean up and put all my stuff in a carry-on. I took a cab to the airport. When you're on an expense account, you can fly anytime and anyway you want. Especially, when your client just fell into a fifty-million-dollar estate. I booked first class and slept half the way back to Miami.